D0975671

Everyone searches for paradise,

but not everyone knows where to look. . . .

Geronimo Stilton

THE QUEST FOR PARADISE

THE RETURN TO THE KINGDOM OF FANTASY

Scholastic Inc.

New York   Toronto   London   Auckland

Sydney   Mexico City   New Delhi   Hong Kong

ISBN 978-0-545-25307-9

Based on an original idea by Elisabetta Dami.

www.geronimostilton.com

Published by Scholastic Inc., 557 Broadway, New York, NY 10012. SCHOLASTIC and associated logos are trademarks and/or registered trademarks of Scholastic Inc.

Stilton is the name of a famous English cheese. It is a registered trademark of the Stilton Cheese Makers' Association. For more information, go to www.stiltoncheese.com.

Text by Geronimo Stilton
Original title *Secondo Viaggio nel Regno della Fantasia: Alla Ricerca della Felicità*
Cover by Iacopo Bruno
Illustrations by Francesco Barbieri, Silvia Bigolin, Federico Brusco, Lorenzo Chiavini, Michele Dallorso, Andrea Denegri, Valentina Grassini, Blasco Pispia, Vittoria Termini, Anna Ziche, and the Piemme Archives
Graphics by Merenguita Gingermouse, Zeppola Zap, Sara Baruffaldi, and Yuko Egusa

Special thanks to Kathryn Cristaldi
Translated by Julia Heim
Interior design by Kay Petronio

23 22 21 20 19   17 18 19 20 21/0

Printed in China
First printing, October 2010   38

THE HEART-FINDERS CLUB

THE DRAGON OF THE RAINBOW: I am the faithful messenger of Blossom, the Queen of the Fairies. I like to sing and breathe fire (not at the same time, of course). I also love to get my ears scratched. Ahh! There's nothing like a good scratch!

GOOSE BLAHBLAH: I am a nurse. I also like to talk a lot. In fact, people call me a big blabbermouth, but I don't care. Do you have a few hours? Let me tell you about when I was a gosling. . . .

BOILS: I'm a little boil-covered chameleon. I used to work as a spy for the stinky trolls before I got the gig with Geronimo. Now I'm his guide in the Kingdom of Fantasy.

GERONIMO STILTON:
I run *The Rodent's Gazette*,
the most famouse newspaper
on Mouse Island. I like to
write about all my fabumouse
adventures — especially my
adventures in the Kingdom
of Fantasy!

SNOWY DAWN: I am the
Princess of the Snow, daughter
of the Ice King. I am always
sad. I lost my family long ago,
and now I do not speak.

OSCAR ROACH: I am a
cockroach, and I was born
in Roachville. I can cook,
dance, play the violin, and
tell jokes.

ROCKET: I am a unicorn,
but I also have a pair of
wonderful wings. With my
magical wings, I can zoom
through the sky as fast
as a rocket!

I AM JUST AN
ORDINARY MOUSE....

I am just an ordinary mouse. But I have had some **EXTRAORDINARY** adventures — adventures that will curl your whiskers! This story takes place in a *strange* and **magical** land called the Kingdom of Fantasy.

Oh, how could I *forget*? I haven't introduced myself yet. My name is Stilton, *Geronimo Stilton*. I run a newspaper, THE RODENT'S GAZETTE, in a place called New Mouse City.

This is
The Rodent's
Gazette!

And this is me, Geronimo Stilton!

A GREAT IDEA

It was a normal evening, around dinnertime. I was HURRYING home from work. I couldn't wait to eat the tasty cheese casserole I had made. But just then I ran into my ANNOYING cousin Trap.

"Geronimoid!" he squeaked. "Have I got some EXCITING news for you!"

"What is it?" I asked suspiciously. I'm always wary around my cousin. That's because he likes to play tricks on me.

"My FIRST NEWS FLASH is . . . tonight, I'm opening a restaurant!" he announced.

"Great idea," I said, thinking just the opposite. My cousin is an AWFUL cook.

"My SECOND NEWS FLASH is . . . there will be a show for the grand opening. A **very special** mouse will attempt to beat the WORLD RECORD FOR STUFFING YOUR FACE by eating more than ONE HUNDRED plates of spaghetti!" he continued.

"Great idea," I said, thinking just the opposite. What kind of a **nut** would stuff his face like that?

"And my THIRD NEWS FLASH is . . . *the rodent who will try to break the RECORD is* **YOU**!"

"Great idea," I said, without thinking. Then it **hit** me.

BAD IDEA! BAD IDEA! I thought. But it was too late to say it out loud. I had already fainted.

When I came to, Trap was busy COMBING my fur. "No need to thank me, Cuz," he said. "I know you want to look good for the cameras."

"C-c-c-ameras?" I stammered.

My cousin grinned. "Of course, Gerrykins. Thanks to me, THOUSANDS — no, millions ... no, Billions — of mice all over the world will see you. I invited all the journalists and all the photographers and all the television reporters on MOUSE ISLAND! They were very interested. Everyone wants to see you make a pig of yourself!" He smirked.

Geronimo will beat the WORLD RECORD FOR STUFFING YOUR FACE!

Uhhh? Whatwhatwhat?

Really?

I felt sick and I hadn't even taken one **nibble** of spaghetti! Oh, how did I get into such a **mess**?

"But, Trap, you know I have a weak stomach," I whined. "I'll **never** be able to do it!"

My cousin rolled his eyes. "Oh, don't be such a *wimp*," he scoffed. "You *love* spaghetti, and my restaurant needs the publicity! You have to do it!"

I chewed my PAWNAILS. I was about to scamper away when someone grabbed my tail. When I looked up, two *violet-colored* eyes were staring back at me. They belonged to my sister, *Thea*.

The Stilton Family

Thea Stilton
Geronimo's sister
Special correspondent for *The Rodent's Gazette*. She flies her own airplane, rides a motorcycle, and loves adventures.

Trap Stilton
Geronimo's cousin
His dream is to open a restaurant. He tells awful jokes and loves to play pranks — especially on Geronimo!

Benjamin Stilton
Geronimo's nephew
He's super-sweet. When he gets older he wants to be a journalist, just like his uncle Geronimo.

"What's up, Little Brother? Are you about to **SCAMPER**?" Thea asked.

I groaned. I was like a mouse caught in a maze.

Then I felt a paw **tugging** at my sleeve. "Uncle! Are you really going to beat the WORLD RECORD FOR STUFFING YOUR FACE? That's so **AWESOME**!" my nephew squeaked.

I sighed. That did it. I told Trap to start his stopwatch. You see, I can **NEVER** say no to my *dear* nephew Benjamin. Trap brought me my first plate of spaghetti. "You have one hour to break the **WORLD RECORD**!" he announced.

And so I began. . . .

Geronimo Stilton and
THE WORLD RECORD FOR STUFFING YOUR FACE!

I PLATE OF SPAGHETTI...

10 PLATES OF SPAGHETTI...

20 PLATES OF SPAGHETTI...

30 PLATES OF SPAGHETTI...

40 PLATES OF SPAGHETTI...

50 PLATES OF SPAGHETTI...

60 PLATES OF SPAGHETTI . . .

70 PLATES OF SPAGHETTI . . .

80 PLATES OF SPAGHETTI . . .

90 PLATES OF SPAGHETTI . . .

101 PLATES OF SPAGHETTI: NEW WORLD RECORD FOR STUFFING YOUR FACE!

A FURRY BEACHED WHALE

By some miracle, I managed to beat the WORLD RECORD FOR STUFFING YOUR FACE. I would have patted myself on the back, but I was so STUFFED I couldn't reach my back anymore. I **rolled** all the way home.

When I got home, I made myself a HUMONGOUS cup of chamomile tea. I felt like a **furry** beached whale. After my tea, I crawled into bed.

chamomile tea

I fell into a deep sleep.

But at exactly **midnight**, a strange sound woke me. . . .

Laa! Laa! Dee! Da! Laa! Laa! Dee! Da!

I sat up and grumbled. Who was *singing* outside my open window? Didn't they know what time it was? I was about to tell the mad singer to get lost when I noticed two enormous GOLDEN **eyes** in the **dark** sky. Then I smelled the scent of roses.

Cheese niblets! It was the **Dragon of the Rainbow**!

Do you know the dragon? I met him on my last adventure through the *Kingdom of Fantasy*.

"Greetings, Sir Geronimo! I have brought a message from *Blossom*, the Queen of

What???

the Fairies!" the Dragon of the Rainbow sang. Then he presented me with an official-looking scroll.

I have to admit, I was so **EXCITED** my eyes nearly popped out of my fur. I mean, it's not every day a mouse hears from the Queen of the Fairies.

THE DRAGON OF THE RAINBOW

is the messenger of the Queen of the Fairies. His body is covered in gold scales and he has seven horns that are the colors of the rainbow. He loves classical music and a good scratch behind the ears. He sings when he speaks and is as strong as a thousand dragons.

The scroll was written in **Fantasian**, the language of the Kingdom of Fantasy. I quickly translated it.

It seemed the queen needed me.

"I must leave at once!" I squeaked, changing out of my pajamas and fluffy slippers. I hoped I sounded **BRAVE**. After all, everyone in the Kingdom of Fantasy thought I was a **Fearless** knight!

Can you translate the message from the Queen of the Fairies?

HERE IS THE FANTASIAN ALPHABET!

TO THE RAINBOW!

I started to climb onto the dragon's back. Then I stopped. I had to go to the bathroom. How embarrassing! How humiliating!

   After I returned from the bathroom and was safely settled on the dragon's back, we took off. His golden wings lifted us into the sky.

My whiskers trembled. Part of me was super-excited. I couldn't wait to return to the Kingdom of Fantasy. The other part of me was terrified.

Did I mention I'm terribly afraid of heights?

I wondered if the dragon had ever thought of installing a seat belt, but I didn't think it would be polite to ask. So I took a deep breath and tried to relax.

I had to admit, the dragon was an expert flier.
He glided through the night sky easily, gently
flapping his wings. And his body was as soft as a
pillow.

IN THE KINGDOM OF FANTASY!

After a while, I started to feel sleepy. Then the Dragon of the Rainbow began to sing:

Rest your head, O gentle knight,
Soon the day will bring its light.
But for now the stars will shine,
And everything will be just fine!

I know it's hard to believe I could fall asleep on the back of a *flying* dragon, but I did.

I woke up at dawn to the sound of my own snoring. HOW EMBARRASSING!

The sun was just beginning to rise in the sky. Cautiously, I looked down. What an amazing sight! We had reached the Kingdom of Fantasy!

There was the scary **KINGDOM OF THE WITCHES**,

Magic and Fantasy

Though they are often confused, magic and fantasy are two very different things. . . .

MAGIC IS AN ILLUSION. A magic wand is not enough to change reality or to transform things. Many have tried to use magic to solve problems, but magic does not really exist — it's always just a trick of the eye.

FANTASY IS A POSITIVE ABILITY. Those who are imaginative can see the world with different eyes. They see things that others cannot. If you have a problem, try to resolve it in an *imaginative* way by looking at it from another point of view. You can use your creativity, initiative, and optimism to solve most problems!

where Cackle, the Queen of Darkness, reigns.

Then there was the **Kingdom of the Mermaids**, where many dolphins and sea serpents lived.

Giant

The gloomy **KINGDOM OF THE DRAGONS** is a dry stretch of volcanic rock inhabited by **FIRE-BREATHING** dragons.

Gnome

Mermaid

I had also been to the funny **Kingdom of the Pixies**, where you can have fun with a thousand riddles.

In the **Kingdom of the Gnomes**, nature is always protected.

Witch

Pixie

And the freezing **Kingdom of the Giants** is the home of the last of the giants.

Dragon

Fairy

Fountain of Youth

Valley of the
Blue Unicorns

Finally, I spotted the colorful *Kingdom of the Fairies.*

The air smelled like *roses.* It was the most **AMAZING** smell in the world. There were lots of **COOL** places in the Kingdom of the Fairies.

We passed over the **Fountain of Youth**, the **Valley of the Blue Unicorns**, the House of the Sun and the Moon, the House that Sings, and the **Fairy Godmother's Tower**.

House of the Sun
and the Moon

House that Sings

Fairy Godmother's Tower

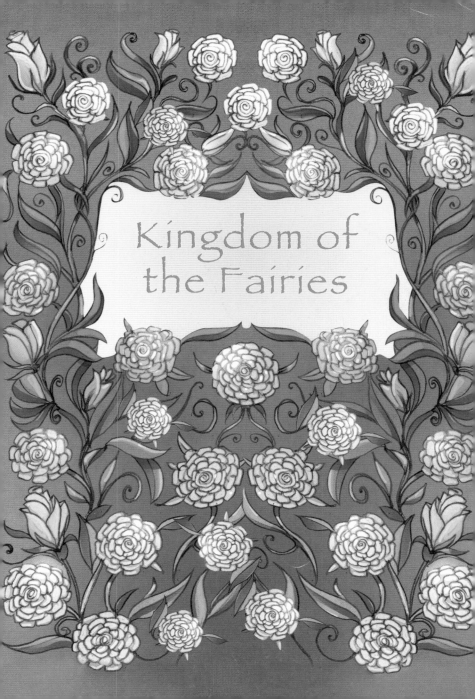

Kingdom of the Fairies

1. ROSE OF A THOUSAND PETALS
2. GLITTERING LAKE
3. WOODS OF GOODNESS
4. PRETTY-SHADE PLAIN
5. PINK FOREST
6. TOOTH FAIRY'S MANOR
7. TURQUOISE HOUSE
8. FLOWERY MOUNTAIN
9. SWEET-SMELLING WOODS
10. FOUNTAIN OF YOUTH
11. RARE GLADE
12. HOUSE OF THE SUN AND THE MOON
13. HOUSE THAT SINGS
14. WHISTLING WOODS
15. SILVER ABYSS
16. FAIRY GODMOTHER'S TOWER
17. SILVER-VOICED NIGHTINGALES
18. MOUNTAIN OF SWEET DREAMS
19. VALLEY OF THE BLUE UNICORNS
20. MOUNTAIN OF SECRETS
21. GAZEBO OF LOVE
22. CRYSTAL CASTLE
23. PEGASUS'S ROCK
24. SWEETWATER LAKE
25. FOREST OF THE NYMPHS
26. PETAL WAY

KINGDOM OF THE FAIRIES

FOUR LEGS, A FACE, AND A TAIL!

The Dragon of the Rainbow headed for the CRYSTAL CASTLE, home of *Blossom*, the Queen of the Fairies.

At this point, I was feeling **PROUD** of myself. I was way up in the air and I hadn't had one **panic attack** yet.

Right then, I noticed a **RED** spot running toward us. Or was it a **GREEN**, **BLUE**, or YELLOW spot?

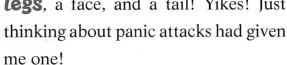

I blinked. Now the spot had **four legs**, a face, and a tail! Yikes! Just thinking about panic attacks had given me one!

Suddenly, the spot began to yell, *"your Excellency!"*

A wave of relief hit me. I wasn't CRAZY.

I would recognize that little voice anywhere. It was **Boils the chameleon**.

We had met on my last visit to the Kingdom of Fantasy. Boils was full of ENERGY — and full of CANDY. He would do anything for sugar!

After we landed, the chameleon ran toward me, breathless.

"Um, do you remember me, Your Knightliness? I'm **Boils**. I'm just a poor boil-covered chameleon, but I am at your service! Everyone has been waiting for you."

I was surprised. "Really?" I squeaked. "They're waiting for *me*?"

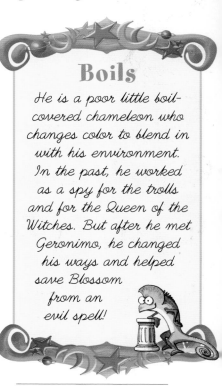

Boils

He is a poor little boil-covered chameleon who changes color to blend in with his environment. In the past, he worked as a spy for the trolls and for the Queen of the Witches. But after he met Geronimo, he changed his ways and helped save Blossom from an evil spell!

Only two of these pictures are the same. Which ones are they?

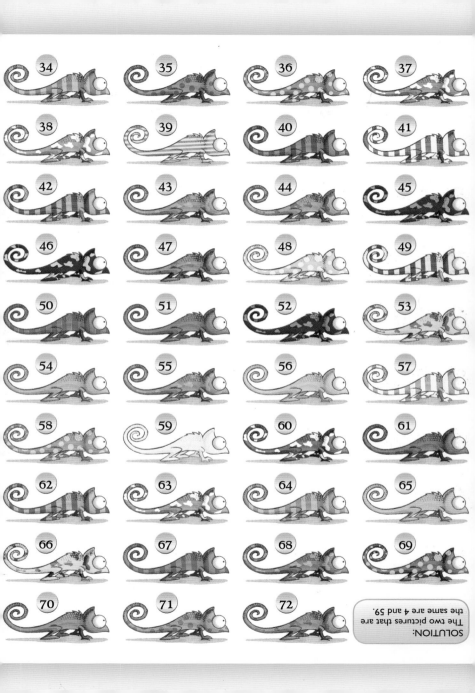

SOLUTION:
The two pictures that are
the same are 4 and 59.

Boils nodded so vigorously his head changed color three times. "Oh, yes, they're waiting for the valiant Sir Geronimo of Stilton to help the queen find her most heartfelt desire."

"And what is that?" I asked.

But Boils wouldn't say. "The queen will have to fill you in on that one, Sir Geronimo," he said. "It's a **BiG**, **BiG** secret."

I gulped. Talk about putting pressure on a mouse! How was I, a newspaper mouse, supposed to help the queen find her most heartfelt desire? And what could it be, anyway? Would I have to travel through strange and DANGEROUS lands?

This is me, Boils!

Official Guide of the Kingdom of Fantasy

Would I have to battle evil monsters? Would I have to give up my nightly BUBBLE BATH?

"Let's go," I told the chameleon. I was as CURIOUS as a whole litter of kittens!

Boils licked his lips. He seemed to be waiting for something.

"You wouldn't by any chance happen to have a small candy for a *poor little boil-covered* chameleon?" he asked.

I should have known! I'm telling you, that lizard must have sugar in his veins!

I found a piece of candy for Boils and then we were off.

Before long, we had reached the shimmering CRYSTAL CASTLE. Boils announced our arrival. The door opened and we headed down a longggggggggggggggggggggggggggggggggggg hallway.

Ooooooh!

Here is the castle of the Queen of the Fairies!

THE QUEEN
OF THE FAIRIES

I brushed against the crystal of the castle. It was **cool** and **warm** at the same time. It was **TRANSPARENT**, but it also **SHIMMERED** a thousand different **colors**. It felt **soft** and yet it felt **hard**, too. How odd!

Then I looked down and saw something even stranger. Boils had become **TRANSPARENT**! Yes, you could see right through him! Well, I guess it wasn't really that strange, considering he's a chameleon, but he sure looked **funny**.

I tried not to laugh, but it was hard. He looked like a walking **icicle**. I shoved a candy into my mouth to stop myself from

The Kingdom of the Fairies

Queen: Blossom, the White Queen, Lady of Peace and Happiness, She Who Brings Harmony and Peace

Royal Palace: The Crystal Castle

Currency: Magical florien

Spoken Language: Fairese

Information about the Kingdom: The small, bright fairies who live here dance and sing beautifully. They also use the rays of the sun and moon to weave vibrant fabrics for their precious clothing.

Blossom

giggling, but ended up choking instead. I was hacking away as we approached the queen. How embarrassing!

A string of *fairies* greeted us. One of them saw that I was choking and smacked me hard on the back. The piece of candy *flew* across the room and landed behind a CRYSTAL pillar. How humiliating!

The fairies *giggled*. Then they sang, "Enter, Sir Geronimo!"

In the center of the room was a CRYSTAL throne. Blossom, the Queen of the Fairies, sat facing us.

She was very *small*, with DELICATE skin that shone. Her wings fluttered *softly* on her back. A ring of braided roses adorned her head, and she wore CRYSTAL CLEAR shoes on her feet.

She seemed young and yet WISE.

I bowed shyly. "Your Majesty, I have come," I SQUEAKED. "How can I help you?" I tried to sound like a **courageous** knight.

She smiled. Then she told me she wanted me to go on a **Great Quest** — a quest to find Paradise and bring back the Heart of Happiness.

"Okay," I agreed. "But where is the Heart of Happiness?"

The queen sighed. "The map that will direct

you to the heart can be found in the **Land of the Ogres**. It is called the Map of Paradise. But be careful! The Land of the Ogres is a terribly **dangerous** place," she warned.

Holey cheese! I was scared out of my fur. If the queen says a place is dangerous, it most likely is dangerous. But what could I do? I had *promised* to help. So I took a deep breath, put on my **BRAVEST** face, and nodded.

"Of course, Your Majesty," I said **BRAVELY**. "I will return only when I have found the heart." I hoped she hadn't noticed that my paws were trembling.

At that moment, a chorus of fairies began to sing:

THE HEART OF HAPPINESS IS YOURS TO FIND,
IF YOU ARE STRONG AND TRUE AND KIND.
PICK UP THE KEYS ALONG THE WAY,
AND FOLLOW YOUR OWN HEART EVERY DAY.

WAIT!

I was still feeling nervous when a small voice cried, "Your Excellency, I, **Boils**, will help in the Great Quest! I will be your guide!"

Good idea, I thought. I could use all the help I could get.

"That makes **THREE** of us," I said, counting myself, Boils, and the Dragon of the Rainbow. "Let's call ourselves the Heart-Finders Club."

Suddenly, a **CHUBBY** goose with an *umbrella* raced into the room.

"**WAIT!**" she screeched loudly.

The goose marched up to me. "I am Goose Blahblah.

I am a nurse, Your Knightliness, and I must insist you take me on this trip. I can **help** if someone gets sick. Without me, you'll never make it back **alive**!" she predicted.

I shivered. But Boils **rolled** his eyes. "Oh, puh-lease, GOOSey LOOSe LipS. All of your chattering will drive Sir Geronimo **MAD**. He's taking me!"

Goose Blahblah pinched the chameleon's tail.

"Pipe down, GREEN FACE!" she ordered. "He is going to bring **ME**!"

The two began to argue.

"I'll bring both of you," I said. "That makes **four** of us in the club."

"Actually, there will be **five** of you," the queen said.

Goose Blahblah

Goose Blahblah lives by Sweetwater Lake in the Kingdom of the Fairies. She is a gossip and she is very nosy. She sticks her beak into everyone's business. She is, however, an excellent nurse. She knows all the secrets of medicinal plants and she knows natural remedies to cure any sickness.

THE MOST BEAUTIFUL OF THE BEAUTIES!

A young girl approached us. She was as pretty as a **BUTTERFLY**, and her ‖OOOOONG blond hair looked like *golden* yarn.

Her almond eyes, shaded by ‖OOOOONG eyelashes, were very

THE PRINCESS OF THE SNOW

Snowy Dawn is the daughter of the Ice King. She doesn't speak or laugh. She communicates by writing short messages on small white sheets of paper that look like snow. She lives in the fairies' royal palace. Many suitors have asked for her hand, but none of them have been able to melt her heart of ice.

beautiful, but they were also as cold as ice. Her skin was snowy-white, like a lily, and her ears were SMALL and delicate, like seashells. She was wearing a finely woven dress that billowed with her every step.

Around her neck, she wore a precious jewel shaped like a snowflake.

"This is Snowy Dawn, the Princess of the Snow and the daughter of the Ice King. She is also known as *the most beautiful of the beauties*, and I have decided she will accompany you," the queen said.

I smiled at the princess. "I am honored," I squeaked. I stuck out my paw to shake her hand, but Snowy Dawn didn't move. Instead, she stared at me SILENTLY with those cold eyes. Uh-oh. Was I not supposed to shake her hand? I felt like a fool. I coughed.

"Ahem, well, with you that will make FIVE of

us in the Heart-Finders Club," I stammered.

Snowy just stared.

I gulped. The princess was a beauty, but her icy stare was sort of CREEPY. Why wouldn't she say anything? Was I that APPALLING?

I was dressed in my BEST suit. My teeth were brushed. Maybe she had something against FUR.

Before I could figure it out, the queen patted Snowy on the back. "**Go now!**" she commanded.

At the *queen's* words, Snowy turned suddenly and headed for the door. Behind her, a small sheet of paper *fluttered* to the ground. On it were written these words: *I WILL GO.*

How strange! But there was no time to think about it now. We had to go. Everyone followed me out to the **DRAGON**.

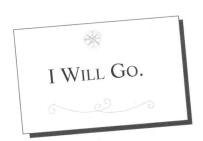

As we walked, Goose Blahblah began **chattering**.

"Don't take it personally," she said. "The princess **never** talks to anyone. In fact, she's known as THE FACE THAT KNOWS NO SMILE and SHE WHO SPEAKS TO NO ONE and THE FROZEN HEART and . . ."

After a while, I stopped listening. Goose Blahblah was the complete **OPPOSITE** of Snowy. She never stopped talking!

ONLY A MEASLY INSECT

Just as we were leaving, a cockroach approached me **excitedly**. "Are you the courageous **HERO** who is going on the **Great Quest** for the Queen of the Fairies? I wish you a good trip, and my  will be with you. My name is **OSCAR ROACH**."

Oscar told me how much he *loved* the queen.

OSCAR ROACH

Born in Roachville, in the far-off Land of the Cockroaches, Oscar Roach arrived in the Kingdom of the Fairies looking for work. He dreams of returning to his homeland one day after making his fortune. He has tried all the jobs in the world and that's why he knows how to cook, dance, play the violin, and tell jokes.

"I know I am only a measly insect, but I would give my life for her," he said earnestly.

I was **IMPRESSED**. After all, it's not every day you meet an insect willing to lay his **LEGS** on the line for someone. Meanwhile, Goose Blahblah was getting **impatient**.

"Geronimo, why are you **WASTING** your time talking to that insect? He's just a **Rotten** bug. Nobody cares about him," she snorted.

I ignored her. I was discovering that besides being loud and a chatterbox, Goose Blahblah could also be **terribly** rude.

The cockroach continued, undaunted. "Oh, how I would love to go with you on the **Great Quest**, Sir Knight," he said wistfully. "I would make myself useful. I would take care of the dragon, **COOK** delicious food, wash the dishes, and do the laundry. And at night I would even play the violin. **Music** always makes everyone happy."

I looked at Oscar. He really seemed like a *charming* bug. He was **sincere** and KIND.

"I've decided that you will come with us," I squeaked. "Welcome to the Heart-Finders Club!"

Oscar was so **EXCITED** he looked like he was about to bust right out of his shell.

Goose Blahblah, on the other paw, was **fuming**. "We're bringing a cockroach?" she whined in my right ear.

"There's no **room** for him," Boils whined in my left.

Only the Dragon of the Rainbow was **HAPPY**. He smiled at Oscar.

Then he sang in a *sweet* voice:

The more hearts we take along,
The more our club grows wise and strong.
So climb aboard, let's go, let's fly,
Into the bright, warm, rosy sky!

Goose Blahblah and Boils were still sulking, so I decided to lead them in a *cheer.*

"**HIP-HIP-HOORAY** for the Heart-Finders Club!" I squeaked.

It worked. Pretty soon we were all cheering.

"Long live the Heart-Finders Club!"

A RAY OF SUNLIGHT hit the castle, making a beautiful **rainbow**.

Then the Dragon of the Rainbow set off.

NO FURBALL
ISLANDS FOR ME!

I settled back and tried to ReLaX. The ride wasn't so bad once you got used to the whole flying-up-high thing. The wind **caressed** my whiskers. I closed my eyes and pretended we were headed for the FURBALL ISLANDS. Have you ever been there? They have the most *beautiful* beaches.

Suddenly, the dragon **dove** left. My eyes flew open. No Furball Islands for this mouse! We were headed for the Land of the Ogres!

The ogres were friends with the **EVIL** Queen of the Witches. I'd met her on my last adventure with my frog friend, SCRIBBLEHOPPER.

It was already evening when Boils yelled, "We're here! It's the Land of the Ogres!"

SCRIBBLEHOPPER

1. Ogre Hill
2. Mount Little Ogre
3. Lazy Louse Trail
4. Stink of Stench River
5. Foul Loaf Mill
6. Spotty Stench Swamp
7. Grubbygrub Village
8. Countess Ogress Lake

9. Hills of the Little Lady Ogres
10. Valley of the Fleabag Fleas
11. Stink Bomb Tower
12. Howling Owl Woods
13. Castle of Nightmares
14. Scab Desert
15. Thorny Thorn Forest

THE LAND OF THE OGRES

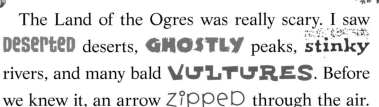

The Land of the Ogres was really scary. I saw **DESERTED** deserts, **GHOSTLY** peaks, **stinky** rivers, and many bald **VULTURES**. Before we knew it, an arrow **ZiPPED** through the air. **Thunk!** It hit the Dragon of the Rainbow. He sang out in pain:

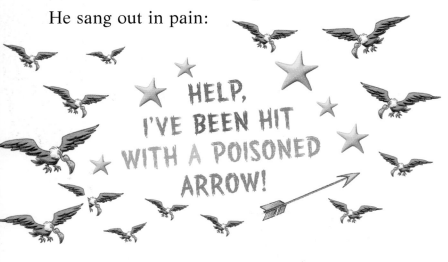

HELP, I'VE BEEN HIT WITH A POISONED ARROW!

Then he plummeted **DOWNWARD** like an airplane with no motor. **Rat-munching** rattlesnakes! What a *disaster*! I held on tight as we fell toward the ground.

We're falling!

The Land of the Ogres

King: Baldsquash, the Great Lord of the Stinkonese Smelloni Stinkers
Royal Palace: Stink Bomb Tower
Currency: Ogero
Spoken Language: Ogrese
Information about the Land:
The ogres are as tall as giants and as dirty as trolls! They are gluttons for fresh meat. Their favorite dish is meatball stew. Their land shares a border with the Kingdom of the Witches. The ogres and witches are friends and allies.

Can you find the CRYSTAL KEY?

THE QUEEN OF THE WITCHES

I stared in horror as the ground grew closer and closer. **YIKES!** We were headed straight for **SpotTy Stench Swamp**! Something hit me in the snout. It was a **CRYSTAL** key. How strange! Then I remembered the fairies **SiNGiNG** something about picking up some keys during our journey. I had no idea what the key was for, but I put it into my **pocket** for safekeeping.

Two minutes later, we sank into the **stinky**, **SLIMY** water. Yuck! I'd really need to hit the cleaners when I got home. I could see thousands of witch faces peeking out from behind the shrubs.

"Oh, great," Goose Blahblah said. "Looks like we've arrived just in time for the **GREAT WITCH GATHERING**."

Boils climbed out of the **MUCK**. "Are you sure it's today, Miss Nosybody?" he muttered.

"Of course I'm sure, *Green Face*!" Goose Blahblah insisted.

The two continued to argue as we swam to the shore, dragging the injured Dragon of the Rainbow behind us.

Suddenly, we heard a scream that made everybody **freeze**.

"**SSSSSILENCCCCCCCCCCCCCCCCE!**"

It was **CACKLE**, the Queen of the Witches. She had **FLAMING RED** hair and a beautiful face. She stared at us with her magnetic almond-shaped eyes. One eye was **BLACK** and the other was **GREEN**.

THE QUEEN OF THE WITCHES

The crows Shriek and Screech are the queen's advisors.

Bambobatty

Mambobatty

Tangobatty

Chubbatty

I **shuddered**. There's one thing you should know about **CACKLE**. She may be *beautiful* on the outside, but on the inside she is pure **EVIL**!

The witches forced us to abandon the poor injured dragon. I felt terrible about it, but we had to follow the witches. "We'll be back soon," I whispered to the DRAGON OF THE RAINBOW. "Hang in there, friend."

The witches took us to a cave where thousands of **BLACK BATS** were hanging. Oh, how I wished I had been curled up at home with a cup of HOT CHEDDAR! Did I mention I'm afraid of bats, witches, and things that go **bump** in the night?

As the witches began to dance, I spotted something in the dirt. It was another KEY. How strange!

Taranbatty

Dancibatty

Humbatty

Singabatty

Can you find the
CRYSTAL
KEY?

THE CAVE OF THE BLACK BATS

Cackle shot me a PIERCING look. "What brings you back, Sir Rodent?" She smirked. "Miss me?"

"It's a big secret," Boils began. "We can't tell anyone about the **Great Quest** —"

"Be quiet, Lizard Brain!" Goose Blahblah interrupted. "You shouldn't tell her that we're on the **Quest for Paradise** or that we're looking for the *Heart of Happiness*!"

Quiet!

No, you be quiet!

Boils threw a fit. "Now look what you've done, Loose Lips! You've **SPILLED** the beans. We weren't supposed to say anything!" he yelled.

"*I* spilled the beans?!" Goose Blahblah retorted. "*You're* the one who couldn't keep his MOUTH shut!"

Before they could go on, Cackle held up her hand.

SSSSSILENCCCCCCCCCCCCCCCE!

she commanded.

 Then she gave me a smile that was sweeter than honey and faker than counterfeit money.

"THE QUEST FOR PARADISE?" she crooned. "The Heart of Happiness? Very interessssssssssting . . ." I knew we had to get out of there **FAST**.

"Your Majesty, will you grant me permission to

TRAVEL through the Land of the Ogres with my, um, **HEART-FINDERS CLUB**?" I asked nicely.

Cackle nodded. "I'll need a feather," she said.

She plucked a feather from an **owl** who was locked in a cage.

Can you find the
CRYSTAL KEY?

At that moment, another CRYSTAL key bonked me on the head.

"**OUCH!**" the owl and I cried out together.

"SSSSSILENCCCCCCCCCCCCCCCCCCCE!" Cackle shrieked.

She dipped the owl's feather in **INK** and began to write on a *scroll*. . . .

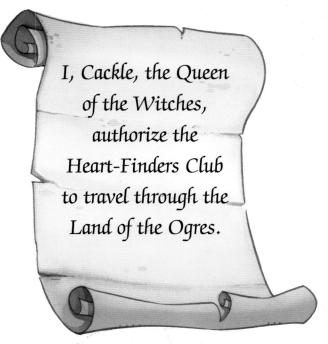

I, Cackle, the Queen
of the Witches,
authorize the
Heart-Finders Club
to travel through the
Land of the Ogres.

I'LL NEVER
FORGET YOU!

While Cackle was busy writing, I spoke quietly
with the owl prisoner. It seemed she'd been locked
up for ten **LOOOONG** years! What could I do?
I had to help her. *Secretly*, I opened her cage.
My paws were trembling. I didn't want to think
about what Cackle would do if she caught me.

The owl FLAPPED her wings. Then she took off for
her home in the **HOWLING OWL WOODS**.

"Thank you!" she called softly. "I'll never
FORGET you!"

As Cackle was stamping the scroll with wax, I found another CRYSTAL key. Strange! I was starting to think I should have brought a large KEY CHAIN with me! I couldn't wait to **leave**. Did I mention that witches really, really **FRIGHTEN** me?

As we were leaving, Cackle whispered something to the **KING OF THE BLACK BATS**. I'm guessing she wasn't asking him for the time, because her SMiLE was pure evil.

A VERY, VERY, VERY EVIL SMiLE!

THREE WITCHES

As soon as we left Cackle, we went searching for the Dragon of the Rainbow.

"We should never have abandoned him," Oscar sobbed.

When we reached the smelly Spotty Stench Swamp, Boils yelled, "Here he is!"

"We found him!" Goose Blahblah shouted.

Snowy Dawn didn't say a word, but she RUSHED to his side.

The dragon had his eyes closed, but his chest lifted and fell slowly. I was relieved he was alive. But he didn't look good. We had to do something to help him.

"What can we do?" I asked worriedly.

As I patted the Dragon of the Rainbow's side, I discovered another KEY on the ground. I was

Can you find the
CRYSTAL
KEY?

getting so used to finding keys I didn't even **BLINK**. I just shoved it into my pocket.

The dragon opened his **EYES** and whispered,

You must go into the Howling Owl Woods,
And find the witches three.
They will have the antidote
That you need to save me!

I was **CONFUSED**. Antidote? Howling Owl Woods? **THREE WITCHES?**

Lucky for me, I had brought Goose Blahblah along. She explained about the three witches who lived in the Howling Owl Woods. They had made the **poisoned** arrow that had hit the Dragon of the Rainbow. Only *they* had the **ANTIDOTE**, the medicine that would **cancel out** the poison.

I gulped. Witches who made poisoned arrows?

I was a nervous **wreck**, but I couldn't let the Dragon of the Rainbow die.

"I'll do it! I'll find the **ANTIDOTE**!" I said,

hoping no one noticed my **shaky** voice.

"Be careful, Your Excellency," Boils warned. "The Three Witches are **gluttons** for fresh meat. They eat travelers that enter their forest."

I opened my eyes **WIDE**. "Eat t-t-t-travelers?" I stammered.

Oscar patted my paw, and Snowy handed me a note.

I was feeling a full-fledged **panic attack** coming on. Tears sprang from my eyes.

BE CAREFUL!

Oh, how had I gotten myself into such a **mess**?

Wah!

Wah! Wah!

I'm scared of the scary witches!

IN THE HOWLING OWL WOODS

I climbed Ogre Hill and entered the HOWLING OWL WOODS. In the darkness, I could see a thousand yellow eyes spying on me. The thorny shrubs pricked at my fur. I tripped over branches and twigs. In the distance, I spotted a river of stinky green water. Gross! Didn't they care about the environment around here?

Right then I realized that someone was following me. It was the KING OF THE BLACK BATS. So that was what Cackle had been whispering about! She had wanted him to follow me. Then I saw something else. I saw the hands of the THREE WITCHES.

Soon I reached the edge of the woods. Can you guess what I found? Yes, another CRYSTAL key!

Can you find the
three hands of the
Three Witches?

SOLUTION: The first hand is on the branch in the top left corner, the second hand is on the branch that juts out of the trunk of the big tree on the left, and the third hand is on the trunk on the right.

That made . . . well, who was counting, anyway? I had **BIGGER** things to think about, like the large tree-stump house in front of me. It had **round** windows that looked like eyes and a door like a sneering mouth! A sign in front read:

The Three Witches' Secret Laboratory

Suddenly, I felt a PINCH on my neck. How strange! I hadn't seen any mosquitoes.

Then I realized I'd been hit by a poisoned arrow! Ouchhhhhhhhhhhhhhhhhhh!

A minute later, I fainted!

Can you find the
CRYSTAL
KEY?

MOUSE SOUP
FOR DINNER!

When I woke up, I was locked in a cage. Three evil voices **screeched**, "We knew you would come. The **KING OF THE BLACK BATS** warned us. Have a nice sleep?"

I stared at the witches. The first one was really **SHORT**. The second one was really **round**. And the third was really **TALL**.

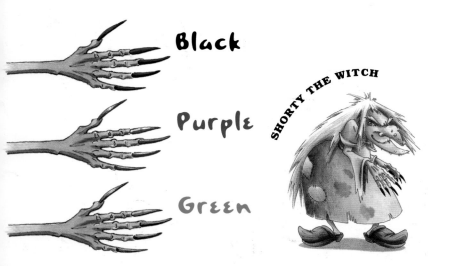

Black

Purple

Green

SHORTY THE WITCH

Shorty had fingernails painted **BLACK**.

Portly had fingernails painted **purple**.

And Stalky had fingernails painted green.

All three had **WHITE** hair, pointy noses, and lots of hairy warts. Let's just say they wouldn't be winning any beauty contests anytime soon.

The Three Witches approached the cage. They took turns PINCHING my tail.

I let out three screams:

"Ow! Oww! Ouch!"

The witches giggled.

STALKY THE WITCH

PORTLY THE WITCH

"Yum yum! Mouse soup **TONIGHT!**" they said.

Shorty lit a **FIRE** under a copper pot.

"I'll gather wood from the **FOREST**," she said.

"I'll get **peppers** for the soup," said Portly.

"And I'll get potatoes for the **side dish**," said Stalky.

The three witches scurried out of the room.

At first I was miffed. Side dish? Wasn't I **enough**? After all, I'm a pretty decent-sized mouse.

Then I smacked my forehead. What was I **THINKING**? I had to escape!

I **grabbed** on to the bars and squeaked,

"**HELP!** Get me out of here!"

As I was rattling the bars, a CRYSTAL key dropped to my feet. Odd. Very odd. Was it the key to the cage? No, it was the wrong size.

Suddenly, I heard a tiny voice. "Do you need a hand, rodent friend?"

It was an owl with large yellow eyes. I recognized her immediately. It was the owl I had saved from QUEEN CACKLE!

"I told you I would **REMEMBER** you. When I saw that you were in trouble, I had to pay you back for your KiNDNeSS and generosity, dear rodent. Be back in a second," the owl said.

Then the owl flew to a hook and got the key to the cage....

DINOSAUR BONES AND YETI FINGERNAILS!

She turned the key in the **LOCK**, and the cage opened.

I was **free**! "Thanks! I **owe** you my life!" I squeaked.

The owl flew to the window. *"Happy to help!"* she called back, disappearing into the **night** sky.

I grinned. This was my chance. I had to find the poison arrow **ANTIDOTE** before the witches returned. I looked around the laboratory. I saw jars filled with dinosaur **BONES**, bats' **WINGS**, frogs' **eggs**, yeti **FINGERNAILS**, and **sprigs** of basil.

SPRIGS OF BASIL

FROGS' EGGS

There also were **vials** filled with

POISON

ANTIDOTE

potions, and many **BOOKS** of spells.

Finally, I found what I was looking for: two bottles. One held a GREEN liquid. It was labeled "poison," and there was a picture of an arrow on the bottle. The other bottle was filled with a **blue** liquid, and it was labeled "ANTIDOTE."

"Jackpot!" I squeaked. Now the Dragon of the Rainbow would be CURED! I was so excited, I completely forgot about the witches.

Just then they barged through the door. Cheese niblets! Without a second to spare, I stuck the bottle into my pocket and **ran**.

The witches chased me, but I kept going. The dragon's life was in my Paws! I crashed past the thorny bushes and stumbled over rocks. My heart HAMMERED in my chest. My fur was drenched in sweat. Did I mention I'm not much of a sportsmouse?

Can you find the
CRYSTAL
KEY?

I climbed up Ogre Hill, past a GREEN stream, and picked up another CRYSTAL key along the way.

At last I arrived at the **Spotty Stench Swamp**. I was dying for a little rest, a drink, maybe even a quick **massage**. But there was no time. The witches were right on my *tail*.

Quickly, I poured three drops of the *blue liquid* into the Dragon of the Rainbow's mouth.

Thank you, Sir Knight. You saved my life!

Can you find the
CRYSTAL
KEY?

AT THE FIRST DROP . . . the dragon opened his eyes.

AT THE SECOND DROP . . . he stretched his mighty wings.

AT THE THIRD DROP . . . he was up and ready to go.

While the Dragon of the Rainbow was recovering, I noticed something **glistening** in the dirt. Those CRYSTAL keys were turning up everywhere! Were they some sort of **clue** to a *riddle*?

I was still thinking about the keys when I heard a sound.

Rancid Swiss rolls! It was Shorty, Portly, and Stalky! They were FUMING!

We jumped onto the dragon's back and he **TOOK OFF** into the sky. We were safe!

IN THE TOWER OF BALDSQUASH THE OGRE

As we were flying, Boils pointed out Stink Bomb Tower, the royal palace of the King of the Ogres. It was surrounded by TALL, SPIKY trees and swarms of insects.

I plucked another KEY from the BRANCHES of one of the trees. How strange!

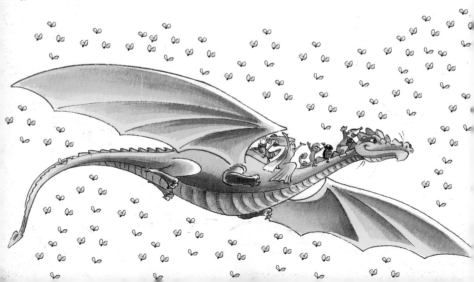

Can you find the
CRYSTAL
KEY?

In the Stinky Land of the Ogres

The Land of the Ogres is very dark and smelly, which is why the ogres chose to live there. The trees have a terrible stench, particularly the ***Arboristincus Vesicleosus***. Instead of flowers and fruit, this tree produces sacs filled with an odorous liquid.

Garlica Grass grows on the ground. When you step on it, it reeks of rancid garlic.

A greenish insect, the ***Smellicolosus Disgustius***, is typical of the region. It is covered with spikes, and when it flutters, it leaves behind a bad-smelling cloud.

Smellicolosus
Disgustius

The water in the rivers is green, dense, and thick and gives off a frightening stench. Very poisonous spiky fish called **Spikiotus Thornatus** swim in the stinky river.

A typical bird is the **Flynatus Stinkerius**.

Spikiotus
Thornatus

Arboristincus
Vesicleosus

Flynatus
Stinkerius

Garlica Grass

Geronimo

The dragon landed on a clearing near the tower.

We decided that I would enter the tower to look for the **Map of Paradise**, while the others would wait outside and stand guard.

I approached the tower on shaky paws. *Oh, please let the map be easy to find*, I thought.

A sign in front of the tower read:

STINK BOMB TOWER

PROPERTY OF BALDSQUASH THE OGRE!

DO NOT ENTER . . . OR I WILL MAKE MEATBALLS OUT OF YOU!

I took a deep breath and knocked.

After a few moments, I felt a terrible tremor.

THUMP THUMP THUMP THUMP!
THUMP THUMP THUMP THUMP!

A woman as tall as a three-story house, with greasy hair, a HUGE nose, and crooked teeth, opened the door. "Who's there?" she bellowed. Behind her were two younger ogres. Unfortunately, the smaller ogres were just as HIDEOUS as their mom. Hadn't anyone ever explained basic hygiene to these creatures?

Still, there was no time for a lesson. I had to get that map.

The ogre didn't see me. I slipped quietly into the house right before she slammed the door.

"Rotten pranksters!" she grumbled.

The ogress STOMPED back into the house. She crossed through the foyer, which was as big as a soccer field. Then she CLOMPED into

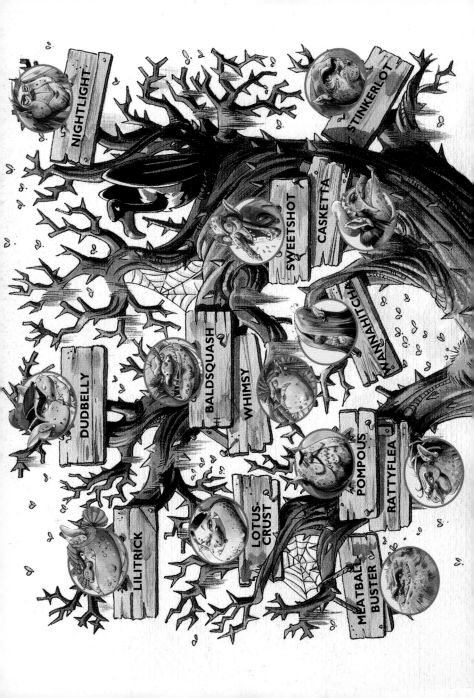

THE ANCIENT FAMILY OF THE OGRES dates back to a long, long time ago, when Sweetbog married Hogbreath and had Stink Bomb Tower built to house her gigantic family. Today some of their descendants still live there. The ogres like fresh meat, which is why if you go to the Land of the Ogres, you should stay away from Stink Bomb Tower!

HAIRHEAD

SNOTBERT

SLAPLOT

SPIDERSTEW

UGLYFLOWER

BUGBAIT

HOGBREATH

SWEETBOG

THE FAMILY OF THE OGRES

WHIMSY

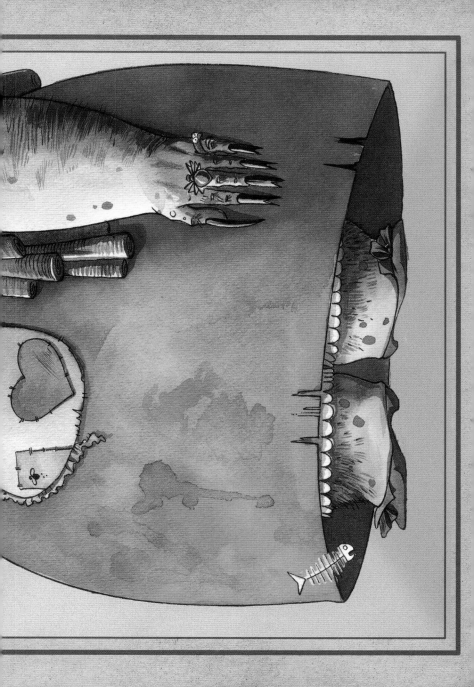

the enormous kitchen and lit a **FIRE** in the fireplace, which was as **BIG** as a truck!

I was hiding under a cupboard when a door **BURST** open.

Holey cheese! The ogre Baldsquash was in the house!

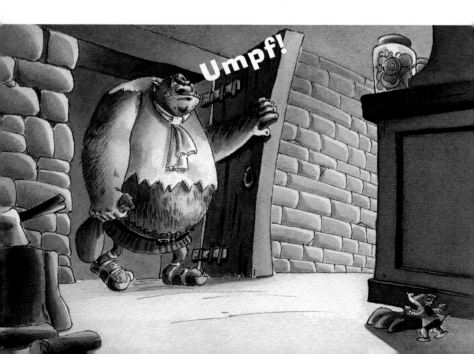

FEE-FI-FO-FAT, I SMELL THE BLOOD OF A NASTY RAT!

"So tell me, **BiG** hubby of mine, how was your **big old** day?" the ogress asked.

"**Umph!** It was pretty big, O large wife of mine!" thundered Baldsquash in his **EXTRA-LARGE** voice. I began to *shiver* with fear. Plus, it was **freezing** in the kitchen.

Geronimo →

Suddenly, I felt a sneeze coming on. I tried to stop myself, but it didn't work. **"A-CHOO!"**

"Umph!" yelled the ogre. "Who sneezed?"

"It was probably just the **WIND**, big hubby," the

WHAT A HUGE LOAF!

WHAT A GIGANTIC
BOWL OF SOUP!

ogress answered.

I moved and the cupboard **creaked**.

"Umph!" yelled the ogre. "Who made that **creak**?"

"It was probably just the chair you're sitting in, big hubby," said the ogress.

The ogre sniffed the air and an **ugly** look came over his already **ugly** face. "**FEE-FI-FO-FAT**, I smell the blood of a **nasty** rat!" he yelled.

The ogress sighed. "Oh, **big hubby**, it's probably the smell of the **GIGANTIC** soup and **extra-large** meatballs I made," she said.

The ogre **SNIFFED** the air again and **muttered** to himself.

Then he devoured the **GIGANTIC** bowl of soup, which was as **large** as a swimming pool. **Slurp!**

He **MOPPED** up the bowl with a loaf of bread as large as a hot-air balloon.

He pierced an **ENORMOUSE** chunk
of cheese with a super-size fork that looked
just like a pitchfork, and spit out the huge
rind. **Spoo!**

WHAT A
HUGE FORK!

Then he let out a burp that made
the windows shake. **Burp!**

Finally, he cleaned his **HUGE** teeth
using the trunk of a pine tree as a toothpick.
Then he chugged down **thirteen** gallons of
water in a single sip! **Gulp!**

Cheese nuggets, he was **RUDE!**

When he finished eating, the ogre got up and
went to the fireplace.

He knelt down by a large **trunk**. Then
he took an enormous **GOLDEN** key from
his belt, opened the trunk, and pulled out
something.

"Look, Wife, it's my **Map of
Paradise!**" he cried.

SOLUTION: Geronimo is hidden at the foot of the linen chest, near the ogress.

I got out of my hiding place...

I slid the key off his belt...

and I got out of there on tippy-paw!

The ogress **rolled** her eyes. "I know, I know. It's your most **PRECIOUS** possession. Don't lose it," she commanded.

The ogre locked the trunk and **SNIFFED** the air again. "I still smell a rat," he mumbled. A minute later, he was fast asleep.

As soon as I knew that the ogre was asleep, I **SNUCK** out from my hiding place. I **HAD** to get that map!

On tippy-paws I **crept** over the ogre's belly and **SLID** the **GOLDEN** key off his belt.

I was almost at the trunk when the ogre began to mumble in his sleep.

I made it to the trunk and turned the key in the lock. I grabbed the map, but then the heavy lid slammed on my tail!

"**YOUCH!**" I shrieked. So much for being quiet!

The ogre **sprang** from his chair. "Who woke me?" he **thundered**.

Then he saw me. I tried putting on my *friendliest* smile and waving politely. My great-aunt Ratsy always told me everyone likes a **polite** mouse. Unfortunately, she had never met the ogre. He just flew into a rage.

"How dare you enter my

I lifted the heavy lid . . .

I grabbed the map . . .

Then the lid slammed shut on my tail!

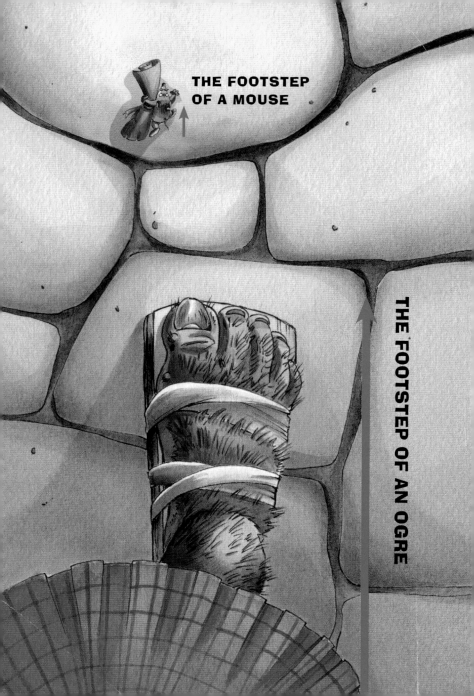

THE FOOTSTEP
OF A MOUSE

THE FOOTSTEP OF AN OGRE

tower?" he bellowed. "I'll gnaw you down to the last TINY BONE!"

Clutching the **Map of Paradise**, I *RACED* for the door.

Too bad the ogre's steps were so much **bigger** than my mouse steps.

"Help!" I squeaked. Was I going to be made into a mouse meatball?

But just as the ogre was about to block my path, I leaped with all my might through the doorway.

With a SWISH, a golden talon lifted me into the air.

"Thanks, Dragon," I squeaked, relieved to be back with my friends again.

The ogre and the ogress shook their fists, but soon they were just two tiNy specks in the distance. At last, we were off to find the Heart of Happiness!

We were off on our   QUEST FOR PARADISE!

THE MAP OF PARADISE!

As we were flying, I showed my friends the **Map of Paradise**. I could hardly believe I was **Finally** holding it in my paws!

"You did it!" Boils yelled. "You got the map!"

"*Yippee!*" Goose Blahblah honked.

Snowy wrote a **NOTE** . . .

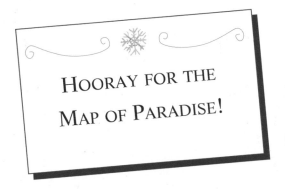

Hooray for the
Map of Paradise!

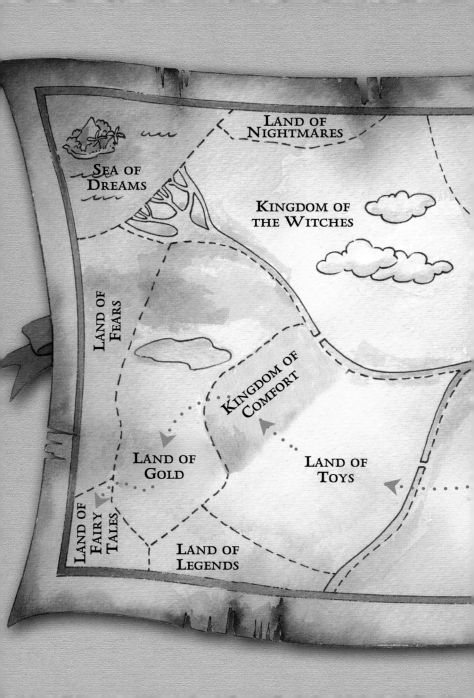

SEA OF
DREAMS

LAND OF
NIGHTMARES

KINGDOM OF
THE WITCHES

LAND OF FEARS

KINGDOM OF
COMFORT

LAND OF
GOLD

LAND OF
TOYS

LAND OF
FAIRY TALES

LAND OF
LEGENDS

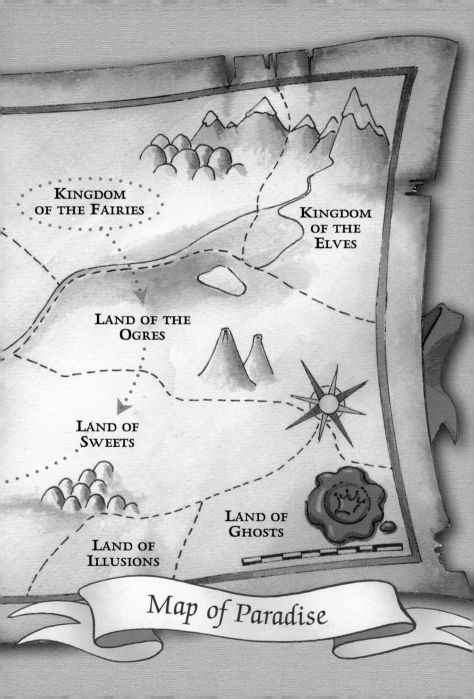

KINGDOM OF THE FAIRIES

KINGDOM OF THE ELVES

LAND OF THE OGRES

LAND OF SWEETS

LAND OF GHOSTS

LAND OF ILLUSIONS

Map of Paradise

Carefully, I unrolled the map and examined it.
The trail began in the *Kingdom of the Fairies*,

continued into the **Land of the Ogres**,

then on to the Land of Sweets,

then to the Land of Toys,

then to the Kingdom of Comfort,

over to the LAND OF GOLD,

and ended in the **LAND OF FAIRY TALES!**

Why didn't I visit these places before?

I was shocked. There were so many **STRANGE** lands on the map. "Why didn't I visit all of these places on my first trip to the **KINGDOM OF FANTASY**?" I asked Boils.

The chameleon *giggled*. Then he *chuckled*. Then he **laughed** until his whole body turned **red**. Finally, he answered me. "Because the **KINGDOM OF FANTASY** is big big big big big big big big big big big big big big big big big big big big big big big big big big big big big big big big big big big big big big big big big big big big big big big big big big big big big big big big big big big big big big big big big big big big big big big big big big big big big big big big big big big big big big big big big big big big big big big big big big big!"

"Oh, yes, oh, yes," agreed Oscar Roach. "The Kingdom of Fantasy is **SUPER-GIGANTIC**," he said.

"He's absolutely right, Your Excellency," said Goose Blahblah. "It's the **biggest** kingdom of them all!"

I was **DEEP** in thought when suddenly Boils screamed, "**LANNND! LAAAAANNNNNNND!**"

Right then I caught a whiff of **chocolate**. We were flying over the **Land of Sweets**.

Chocolate!

The Land of Sweets

1. ICE CREAM MOUNTAIN
2. COCOA VOLCANO
3. CHOCOLATE CASTLE
4. COOKIES AND CREAM MOUNTAIN
5. GLUTTON CITY
6. CREAM PUFF HILL
7. SWEET RAISIN WOODS
8. PASTRY PLAIN
9. MARZIPAN VILLAGE
10. LEMONADE LAKE
11. SPONGE CAKE FOREST

12. INDIGESTION RIVER
13. NOUGAT TOWER
14. WHIPPED CREAM MOUNTAIN
15. SLUSHY PEAK
16. ORANGE JUICE SPRING
17. CAVITY CAVE
18. MERINGUE MOUNTAIN
19. CONFETTI STEPS
20. CARAMEL DESERT
21. CANDY-COATED CITY
22. BLACK CHERRY VALLEY

THE LAND OF SWEETS

A CANDY-COATED CITY!

It was already sunset when the dragon began his slow DESCENT into the Land of Sweets. What an amazing place! There were rivers of *orange soda*, lakes made of **fruit juice**, and a glacier made of mint slushy.

The land was inhabited by little men and women made of *cookies*.

The Land of Sweets

Queen: Her Sweetest Majesty Chocolatina, Empress of the Glutton, Queen of All That Is Gluttonous, Princess of Bonbons, Duchess of Sugariness, Lady of Tummy-aches
Royal Palace: Chocolate Castle
Currency: Cookieso
Spoken Language: Candese
Information about the Land: The inhabitants of this land are made of cookies! They have caramel hair and marzipan mouths.

There was a volcano that shot out a **BLAST** of melted **chocolate**.  And there was a **LAKE** with a graham cracker boat. A candy plane soared over **PUFFED SUGAR** clouds.

 The dragon landed in the **CANDY-COATED CITY!**

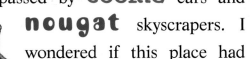 We passed by **cookie** cars and **nougat** skyscrapers. I wondered if this place had any chocolate Cheesy Chews. My favorite!

Just then I tripped over something on the ground. Was it a **GUMDROP**? A **peppermint**? A **caramel**? No, it was another **CRYSTAL** key.

SWEETS

LOLLIPOPS

CHOCOLATE WAY

BIRTHDAY CAKES

Can you find the
CRYSTAL
KEY?

A GINGERBREAD MAN AND AN EDIBLE HOUSE

We left the CANDY-COATED CITY and entered the SPONGE CAKE FOREST.

Of course, Boils was in *heaven*. There was nothing that chameleon *loved* more than candy!

He sucked on lollipop flowers and splashed through the LEMONADE LAKE. "Look at all the little bubbles!" He giggled.

Finally, we arrived at **MARZIPAN VILLAGE**.

Boils ran toward a gingerbread house and began chomping away. I was about to tell him to stop when I noticed another CRYSTAL key. How strange.

At that moment, a *gingerbread man* stuck his head out the window. "Hey,

Can you find the CRYSTAL KEY?

Chomp!
Chomp!
Chomp!

stop eating my **HOUSE**!" he yelled.

Boils licked a **crumb** from his mouth. "Just one more little taste," he insisted.

He **CHOMPED** away at the house until he collapsed into a heap. *Chomp! Chomp! Chomp! Plop!*

"Whew!" Boils exclaimed, rubbing his belly. "I think I ate fifty pounds of *gingerbread*, three hundred **cookies**, seventy **lollipops**, and at least two tons of **caramel**!" He let out a loud burp.

While we waited for Boils to finish burping, Oscar picked up a *heart-shaped* candy. He gave it to Snowy. "This is for you," he said. "I hope it will make you *happy*."

Goose Blahblah rolled her eyes. "A **candy** heart? Who wants that? Now, I'll tell you what would make a girl happy. How about a nice

diamond necklace or a *fancy* hat or a house or a sports car or a . . . ," she babbled.

We checked into a **candy** hotel. It had a SPONGE CAKE bed, a **lollipop** desk, and a **chocolate** lamp. What was hanging from the lamp? A CRYSTAL key!

NO WAY!

The next day, Boils looked extra-green. "Oh, what a stomachache!" he moaned.

Goose Blahblah shook her head. "You ate too many SWEETS, Lizard Breath. Here, drink this smelly pink stuff. It will make you feel better," she said.

"No way!" Boils shrieked.

Then he started moaning again. "Oh, what a toothache!" he cried.

Goose Blahblah grabbed her TWEEZERS. "You've got a cavity. Let me pull your tooth out," she demanded.

"No way!" Boils yelled.

As the two were arguing, Oscar and I studied the **Map of Paradise**.

"Tomorrow we'll need to leave early to

reach the *royal palace* and meet **Queen Chocolatina**," he said.

The royal palace sat on top of **Cookies and Cream Mountain**. Oscar explained that it would be very **cold** and we would need mountain-climbing gear.

But when we went to find the gear, we discovered that everything was made of **candy**, even the jackets, the boots, and the ropes!

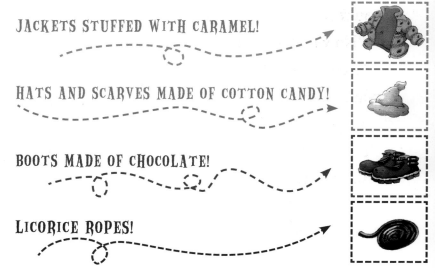

JACKETS STUFFED WITH CARAMEL!

HATS AND SCARVES MADE OF COTTON CANDY!

BOOTS MADE OF CHOCOLATE!

LICORICE ROPES!

We left at **dawn** to begin the climb up **Cookies**

and Cream Mountain. I dragged myself out of my COMFY sponge cake bed and brushed my teeth. Oh, how I HATE to get up in the morning! I felt like I was still half asleep. Then I stepped outside.

Holey cheese, it was cold! In two minutes, my whiskers were covered in icicles!

We began marching through the snow, up and down, up and down, up and down, up and down. We marched all day long.

In the evening we stopped to sleep. We lit a FIRE. We melted some of the cookies-and-cream ice to drink. I must say, I felt like a real MOUNTAIN CLIMBER.

Up and down and up and down and up and down and up and down and up and down and up and down and up and down!

Before I went to bed, I brushed my teeth with the last drop of water from my canteen. Even mountain climbers need **bright** smiles!

Then I found another CRYSTAL key. Good thing I had **deep** pockets. I had collected enough keys to open my own key shop!

Can you find the CRYSTAL KEY?

THE HALF-FROZEN CLUB!

The next day we continued climbing **Cookies and Cream Mountain**.

It was getting **COLDER**. And I could tell everyone was exhausted.

Forget the Heart-Finders Club. We looked more like the **Half-Frozen Club**!

"I have an idea," I said. "How about we have a contest to see who can tell the funniest joke?"

Oscar began:

A family of little tomatoes is walking down the street. The dad notices that the littlest tomato is lagging behind, so he yells, "Ketchup!"

Everyone rolled on the ground, they were **laughing** so hard!

Well, everyone except Princess Snowy.

She just stared into SPACE.

"That one has no sense of **HUMOR**," Goose Blahblah observed.

But Oscar defended her.

"She'll come around," he said confidently. "She just needs a little TIME. Now, who's next?"

Boils JUMPED up. "Me! Me!" he shouted. And so he began:

Why didn't the lobster share his plankton with his dad?

Because he was a little shellfish!

Everyone **applauded**. "Good one, Boils!" we cried.

Next it was Goose Blahblah's turn.

A mother snake bought a gift for her son's birthday. The son was so thrilled he hissed, "Mommy! Help me open it. I'm crawling out of my skin with excitement!"

We all chuckled at that.

When it was my turn, I asked, "Does anyone know this one?"

What did the banana say to the judge?

I'll be sure to win my case on a-peel!

Everyone was giggling so much that the Dragon of the Rainbow also wanted to take part in the contest. He even had **TWO** silly jokes to share!

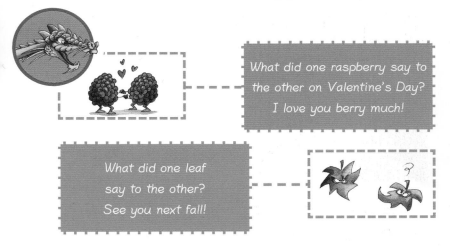

What did one raspberry say to the other on Valentine's Day? I love you berry much!

What did one leaf say to the other? See you next fall!

Boils was laughing so hard he began rolling around in the snow.

"Those jokes were **so funny**!" he shrieked. He laughed so hard he started turning **BLUE**.

Then he rolled . . . right off a **CLIFF**!

Ha ha ha!
He he he!
Ho ho ho!

I'm a Scaredy-Mouse!

Cheese niblets! I looked over the **cliff** and yelled, "*Boilsssssssssssssssssssss!*" but there was no answer.

"We have to get him!" Oscar cried.

Goose Blahblah just snorted. "He should have been more **CAREFUL**. Who rolls around right near the edge of a cliff? Doesn't he have any sense? I always say . . ."

But I wasn't listening. I was **SCARED** out of my fur, but I knew what I had to do. With shaky paws, I tied a rope around my middle. Carefully, my friends lowered me down the cliff side.

On my way down, I picked up another CRYSTAL key. Strange how those keys showed up during the oddest times!

By now my whiskers were shaking with fright. I don't know if you know this about me, but I'm a bit of a scaredy-mouse. Well, okay, I'm not a bit of a scaredy-mouse. I'm a complete scaredy-mouse! In fact, sometimes I'm afraid of my own shadow! But even though I was scared, I had to help Boils.

All of a sudden, I heard a loud creak!

"Hurry, Geronimo!" Oscar warned. "The hole is CAVING IN!"

Finally, I reached the bottom.

I tied Boils to the rope and yelled to the others to pull him up. After the chameleon was safe, it was my turn to climb.

The walls around the hole continued to creak.

I climbed with every bit of **STRENGTH** I had left in me.

I jumped out just as the ice was closing up the hole. Made it by a *whisker*!

What a **fabumouse** ending!

As I gave Boils a **big** hug, I found another **KEY**.

Can you find the **CRYSTAL KEY?**

It's great . . .

to be friends!

IN THE
QUEEN'S COURT

At last we spied the royal palace: **Chocolate Castle**!

We followed a peanut brittle path right up to the castle, which was decorated with CANDY.

All around the castle was a moat filled with a golden liquid.

I slipped and soon discovered that the moat was filled with sticky honey!

A guard made of **COOKIE** poked his head out a window. When he saw us, he lowered the **chocolate** drawbridge.

A row of guards exclaimed, *"Who are you?"*

Who... are you? What... do you want? Why... are you... here? Where... do you... come from?

Can you find the
CRYSTAL
KEY?

Um, honey?

I climbed out of the moat. Honey **dripped** out of my ears. I wiped my glasses and noticed that a CRYSTAL key was stuck to one lens.

I knocked on the *licorice* door. "My name is *Geronimo Stilton*," I squeaked. "I'm here with the Heart-Finders Club, and I'd like to meet the Queen of Sweets!"

Two guards appeared and led us inside. "I see you took a **SWIM** in our moat," one chuckled. "Pretty **clever**, eh? We use it to keep the thieves away."

I didn't think it was very clever, considering I wasn't a thief. I was a **gooey** mess! Oh, what I would have given for a nice HOT bath with **cheddar-scented** bubbles!

great licorice doors

The guards insisted that the dragon stay on the balcony. The last time he'd visited the castle, his FIRE breath had melted the chocolate hall!

a fountain with pink syrup

The rest of us followed them to a room with a fountain that squirted PINK SYRUP. And what was floating inside the fountain? Another CRYSTAL key! I put it into my pocket before anyone noticed.

Then I bowed before Queen Chocolatina. "Excuse me, Your Sweetness. Do you know where I can find the Heart of Happiness?" I asked.

The queen thought for a minute. "I will tell you, but first you must pass a TEST," she said at last.

A VERY
DIFFICULT TEST!

The queen licked her lips.

"I must warn you, it is a very **DIFFICULT** test. You must make me a sweet that I have **never** tasted before. But be careful, because I know all the sweets in the world!" she said.

I chewed my whiskers. Don't get me wrong: I **love** sweets as much as the next mouse. But I can't make them. Then I thought of the one dessert I could make. It's called **Cheesyful Cake**, and it was created in New Mouse City.

I **whipped** up a cake and presented it to Chocolatina.

The whole court watched as she tasted it.

I felt **FAINT**.

What if she didn't like it?

Suddenly, the queen stood up. Then she **THREW** the cake into the face of the royal cook!

"Why didn't you ever make me this cake from Mouse Island?!" she screeched.

"WHY? WHY? WHY? WHHHYYYYYYY?"

"B-b-b-but I didn't even know this **M-Mouse Island** ex-existed," the cook *stuttered*.

I felt awful. I didn't want the cook to get in trouble. I explained to the queen that the recipe was a SECRET known only to mice.

The queen forgave the royal cook. "But from now on you must make me this cake **every** day!" she ordered.

Why didn't you ever make me this cake from Mouse Island?

Splaaat!

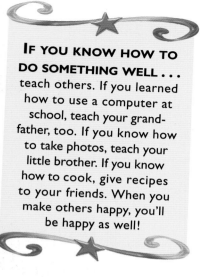

I thought about telling the queen she shouldn't eat Cheesyful Cake every day because it was **loaded** with calories. But I didn't want her screeching, so I kept quiet.

Meanwhile, the cook was so **UPSET** he ran to the kitchen.

"How will I do it?" he **sobbed**. "I've never made this cheesy cake before!"

I told him not to worry. I **wrote** out the recipe. Together we made the cake. The cook was thrilled.

While we were baking, I found another **KEY**. It's a good thing we didn't **bake** it into the cake!

Cheesyful Cake!

Thanks!

CHEESYFUL CAKE

FOR THE CRUST:
- 2 cups graham cracker crumbs, finely ground
- 4 tablespooons sugar
- ¼ cup butter, melted

FOR THE CAKE:
- 4 8-ounce packages of cream cheese, softened
- 1 ¾ cups sugar
- 5 large eggs
- 1 tablespoon vanilla

FOR THE TOPPING:
- 5 tablespoons sugar
- 2 cups sour cream
- 1 teaspoon vanilla
- melted chocolate for design (optional)

Ask an adult to help you make this fabumouse cake!

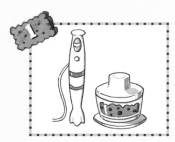

Preheat oven to 350 degrees. Crush the graham crackers in a food processor until very fine. Add butter and sugar. Mix well.

Pour the mixture into a 9-inch springform pan and press it into the bottom of the pan. Bake the crust for 8-10 minutes. Remove pan from oven and set aside to cool.

In a bowl, beat cream cheese, sugar, vanilla, and eggs. Pour the mixture into the pan until it is ¾ full. Bake at 350 degrees about 60 minutes, or until center is firm. Remove cheesecake from the oven.

Combine sugar, sour cream, and vanilla for topping. After the cheesecake has cooled for 10 minutes, spread over top. Return to the oven for an additional 5-10 minutes, or until topping is set.

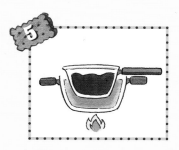

Melt some chocolate in a double boiler. (This step is optional.)

Squeeze or pour the melted chocolate over the cake to make a decoration. For example, you could draw a star, a heart, or some fun squiggles.

Put the cake into the refrigerator until the chocolate solidifies and the cake is set (about 2 hours). Finally, remove cake from springform pan, and enjoy!

THE CHOCO-TREASURE ROOM

After I was sure the royal cook knew the Cheesyful Cake recipe, I went back to talk to the queen.

Now that I had passed her test, **Chocolatina** had promised she would tell me what she knew about the Heart of Happiness. I was feeling *excited*. Could the Heart of Happiness be right here in the *Land of Sweets*?

"It's not here," the queen said a minute later. "But **you** will stay here and cook for me forever!"

I blinked. The queen didn't seem to understand a few things. One: I wasn't a cook. Two: I wasn't a cook. And three: **I wasn't a cook!**

The queen knew I wasn't thrilled about

staying, so she led me to a *secret* room with an
ARMOR-PLATED door.

"Welcome to the chocolate room!" she
announced. She flung open the door.
Inside was the most **fabumouse** sight.
The room was crammed with **chocolate**!
Creamy milk chocolate, **TART** bittersweet
chocolate, and **RICH DARK** chocolate filled
the room.

Then the queen pointed to a huge mountain of
gold chocolate bars.

"This is the choco-treasure. It is made up of
a thousand premium chocolates covered in gold
foil. If you stay here with me, I will give it all to
you," she said.

Oh, no! I was in chocolate heaven! How did the
queen know that chocolate was my **WEAKNESS**?

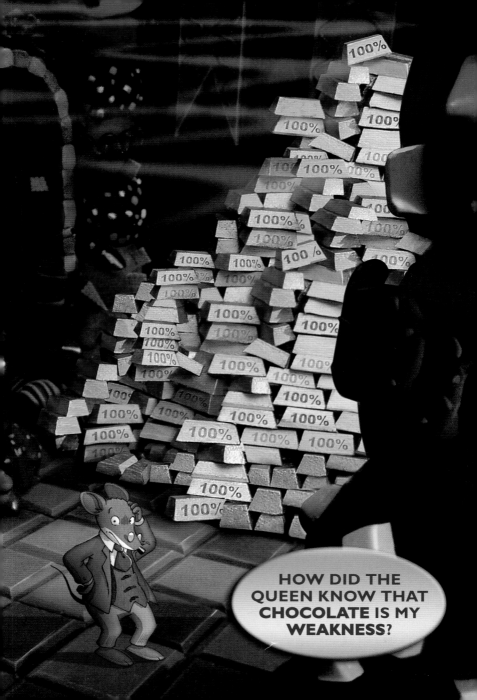

Lucky for me, I didn't have to make a decision. That's because right then, the ground began to tremble. Everyone started screaming.

"The Cocoa Volcano!" the queen shouted. "It's awake!"

We ran out of the castle and jumped onto the dragon just as a **RIVER** of melted chocolate spurted out of the volcano.

"Come back!" Queen Chocolatina called.

But we were already headed toward the

Land of Toys!

THE LAND
OF TOYS

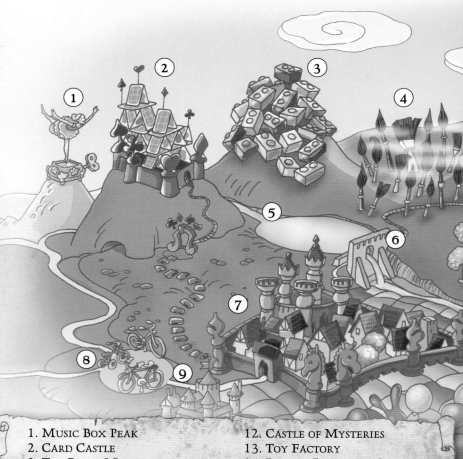

1. MUSIC BOX PEAK
2. CARD CASTLE
3. TOY BRICK MOUNTAIN
4. PAINTBRUSH FOREST
5. WATERCOLOR LAKE
6. SLIDE WATERFALL
7. TOY CASTLE
8. BICYCLE VALLEY
9. TOY SOLDIER FORT
10. CITY OF DOLLS
11. MOUNTAIN OF FUN
12. CASTLE OF MYSTERIES
13. TOY FACTORY
14. ROLLER COASTER OF SHIVERS
15. MODEL TRAIN STATION
16. FOREST OF SWINGS
17. DICE VALLEY
18. SPINNING TOPS LAKE
19. PLASTIC FLOWER WOODS
20. STUFFED ANIMAL CITY
21. ROCKING HORSE TOWN
22. SMILE VILLAGE

THE LAND OF TOYS

LONG LIVE THE LAND OF TOYS!

When we landed in the Land of Toys, I wished I had a pair of sunglasses. It was so BRIGHT and COLORFUL! There were neon green beach balls, PURPLE 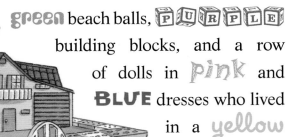 building blocks, and a row of dolls in pink and BLUE dresses who lived in a yellow dollhouse.

Boils jumped onto a toy train.

"Yippee!" he shrieked.
Oscar played

with a **windup** car. And Goose
Blahblah tested
a remote-control

motorboat. Model
airplanes did *loop-dee-loops*
under white clouds.

Then something
fell out of one
plane. Was it
a note? Was it
the pilot? No, it
was just another
CRYSTAL key.

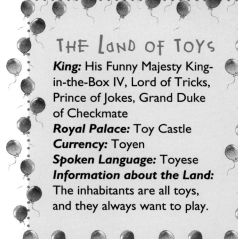

THE LAND OF TOYS

King: His Funny Majesty King-in-the-Box IV, Lord of Tricks, Prince of Jokes, Grand Duke of Checkmate
Royal Palace: Toy Castle
Currency: Toyen
Spoken Language: Toyese
Information about the Land: The inhabitants are all toys, and they always want to play.

Can you find the
CRYSTAL
KEY?

A WOODEN TEAR

As we entered the Land of Toys, I found a trail of what looked like **wooden** tears. How strange! The trail of tears led to a farm.

Inside the barn, a rocking horse was bawling his eyes out.

"Why are you **crying**?" I asked, pocketing a CRYSTAL key I spotted in the barn.

"Oh, my story is a real **tearjerker**," the horse began.

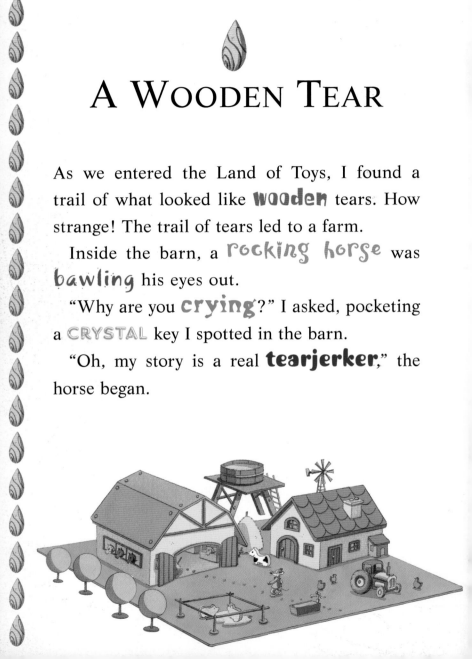

Lightning's Story

My name is Lightning.

Many years ago, toys were not electronic or made of plastic. Children played with cloth dolls, tin trains, and wooden rocking horses just like me.

I belonged to a boy named Peter. He never got tired of playing with me. Together we would pretend I was galloping as fast as the wind. I loved Peter very much.

But eventually Peter got too big to play with me. His mom stuck me in the attic with lots of old furniture.

One day Peter's dad came up to the attic. As he was moving some things, he accidentally broke my rocker, and suddenly, I couldn't rock anymore.

Then Peter's family moved. They didn't want to take all of their old furniture to their new house. So they threw it in the garbage — even me! I dragged myself to this toy farm, which is where I've been ever since.

"Now I'm just an **OLD** piece of wood," the horse finished sadly.

I looked at Lightning. I figured with a little work, we could make him look ten years younger.

"Lightning, it's **makeover** time!" I squeaked.

My friends and I got to work.

We fixed Lightning's rocker, **Painted** his saddle, and **polished** his mane and tail.

The horse was so happy, he couldn't speak. And he wasn't crying any more **WOODEN** tears.

PLAYING TOGETHER

Happiness is not having a lot of toys all for yourself, but sharing your toys with your friends. Try lending your toys to others — it's a good way to make friends!

KING
KING-IN-THE-BOX

We left the farm and headed to our next stop, **TOY CASTLE**.

Two toy soldiers blocked our path.

"My name is Stilton, *Geronimo Stilton*," I said. "I wish to speak with the king."

The guards took us to the royal hall.

As I bowed before **KING KING-IN-THE-BOX**, I found another **CRYSTAL** key and slipped it into my pocket.

"Your Majesty, do you know where I can find the *Heart of Happiness*?" I asked.

The king stared at me. Then he picked up a **magnifying** glass. "What a lovely stuffed animal," he observed.

"Your Majesty, I am not a **STUFFED** animal,"

Can you find the
CRYSTAL
KEY?

What a lovely stuffed animal!

Even the whiskers are top quality!

It can't be synthetic fur!

Put your paws down!

I squeaked. "My name is *Geronimo Stilton*."

The king blinked. "A Stuffed Stilton? Never heard of that brand," he said. "But the quality is EXCELLENT. I don't even see the stitching."

I **fumed**. *Stay calm*, I told myself. *He's just confused*. But the more I tried to explain, the more confused the king became. He **tugged** at my whiskers, convinced they were fake.

Finally, I couldn't take it anymore. "Please just tell me about the Heart of Happiness!" I shouted. The king thought for a minute.

"Okay," he agreed. "But first you must play a game of **chess** with me."

THE GREAT CHESS GAME

A game of chess? Why not? I'd been playing chess since I was a young mouseling. My grandfather William Shortpaws taught me how to play. Of course, he's **SUPERCOMPETITIVE**, so he threw a fit when I beat him, but that's another story. . . .

"Sure," I told the king.

Grandfather William

Good move!

Geronimo

The king showed me an **ENORMOUSE** chessboard. My eyes opened wide. All the pieces were alive!

"I will use the ꟿ𝖧𝖨𝖳𝖤 pieces and you will use the **BLACK** ones," King King-in-the-Box ordered. Then the game began.

A CHESS GAME WITH LIVING PIECES

In 1454, two noblemen fell in love with the beautiful daughter of the Lord of Marostica, a city in the Venezia region of Italy. Since all types of duels were forbidden, the two challenged each other to a game of chess. The event took place in the town square, and the noblemen used living pieces. In 1954, the mayor of the city paved the square to form a chessboard that represented the famous challenge. Since then, a game of human chess is played every two years in Marostica.

Here's How You Play Chess

A chessboard is square: eight columns long and eight rows wide. The chessboard needs to be placed so that the square in the lower right-hand corner facing each player is white.

The player with white pieces goes first.

Placement of the chess pieces
Each piece must be placed inside a square.

IN THE FIRST ROW: At the two ends are the two rooks, next to them are the knights, and next to the knights are the bishops. Place the king and queen at the center. (The queen must be placed in the square that is the same color she is.)

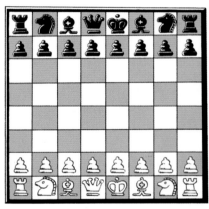

IN THE SECOND ROW: All the pawns are placed here.

How to move the pieces
The pieces must stay inside the boxes and can never be placed between two spaces. With the exception of the knight, they cannot pass through spaces that are occupied by other pieces. They cannot land on spaces that are occupied by pieces on their team. If a piece lands on a space occupied by a member of the opposing team, the player "wins" the piece and takes it off the board. You can win any piece but the king.

King: The king can move in all directions (horizontally, vertically, and diagonally), but the king can move only one square per turn. When the king is trapped and cannot move, it is in "check" and must free itself. If the king cannot free itself, this is called "checkmate," and the game is over.

Queen: The queen can move in all directions (horizontally, vertically, and diagonally) as many squares at it likes, but it cannot go in more than one direction per turn.

 Rook: The rook can move horizontally or vertically (up, down, right, or left) as many spaces as it likes.

Bishop: The bishop can move only diagonally, and it can move as many spaces as it likes.

Knight: The knight is the only piece that can jump over other pieces. It moves in an L shape: two spaces (up/down, right/left) and then one space over, perpendicularly (left or right, up or down).

Pawns: The pawns can move only forward and only one space at a time. However, the first time a pawn moves, it can move two spaces. The space it lands on must be free; otherwise it is won by the opponent. The pawn can only move diagonally if it is winning a piece.

To win the game, you need to get your opponent's king in checkmate!

Remember!

WHATEVER GAME YOU ARE PLAYING IN LIFE, ALWAYS PLAY BY THE RULES!

NO FAIR!

King King-in-the-Box pulled out a **timer**. "You have forty minutes to make your move. If time runs out, you **LOSE** your turn," he said.

That seemed easy. But when I started to make my move, the king tapped me on the back and offered me a *cup of tea*.

"No, thank you," I responded, turning back to the chessboard. Then I noticed something funny. One of my pawns was missing!

"How about some candy?" the king offered.

"No, thank you," I repeated, turning back to the game.

Now one of my knights was missing!

"Pillow?" the king asked, shoving a feather pillow in my snout.

When I pushed it aside, I saw that one of my bishops was missing!

"No fair!" I spluttered. Then I found a CRYSTAL key. Maybe it would bring me good luck.

I studied the chessboard carefully. *Whirling whiskers!* The king might have been cheating, but I had won anyway.

"Checkmate!" I exclaimed with satisfaction. "Now tell me, Your Majesty: Where is the *Heart of Happiness*?"

The king flew into a rage. "How dare you checkmate me? I am supposed to be the **WINNER**!" he shrieked.

He shook his fists in the air. Talk about a sore

Can you find the
CRYSTAL
KEY?

loser! He reminded me of how my cousin Trap was when we were little. We had both entered a sand castle contest and I won. Trap was so jealous, he smashed my castle to **PIECES**.

"It's only a game," I said, but the king was about to **EXPLODE**. I thought about teaching him some relaxation exercises, but I didn't get a chance.

Right then the chess pieces stepped forward. "He won, fair and square!" they told the king.

They explained that the *Heart of Happiness* was not in the Land of Toys.

Then they held the king off so we could make our escape.

IN THE KINGDOM OF COMFORT

We flew to the **Kingdom of Comfort**. Everything in the kingdom was made of something **SOFT**, like cotton or flannel or stuffing.

The houses were sewn, and even the cars were **stuffed**.

We met fabric dolls who wore pajamas and slippers.

"The alarm clocks don't work here, so you can sleep **ALL DAY**," Boils explained.

As I was looking around, I found a **CRYSTAL** key. Maybe it would open up one of the houses. I could have used a bed. I was getting sleepy!

Can you find the
CRYSTAL
KEY?

A man dressed in flannel pajamas offered me a mug of HOT chamomile tea.

"It's so you can sleep better," he said.

I thanked him and climbed up onto a **soft** hill of pillows. As I sipped the tea, my eyes closed.

I slept and slept and slept. It was a total *SNORE-FEST*!

Finally, I woke up. I must say, I could get used to the Kingdom of Comfort. For one thing, I hate alarm clocks. Did I mention that I'm not a morning mouse? And for another, everything was so soft. I couldn't hurt myself. Did I mention that I'm a bit of a klutz?

Still, after a while, even I started to get *bored*.

So we got on the dragon and headed for the Land of Gold.

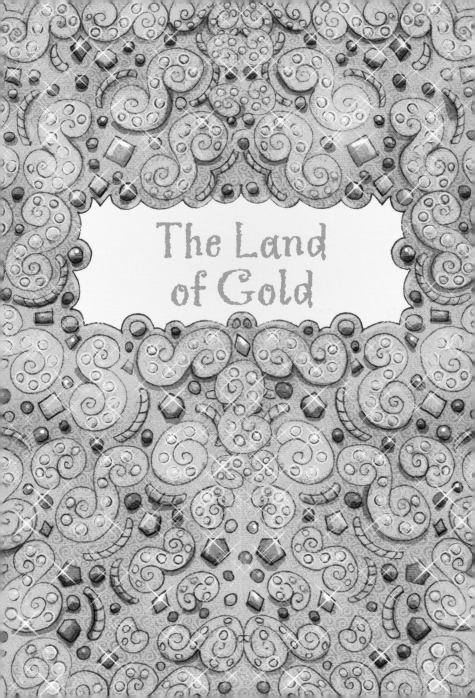

The Land of Gold

THE LAND WHERE EVERYTHING SPARKLES

When we landed, we saw that everything was SPARKLING. Now I really needed those sunglasses. It was so bright! Note to self: Make appointment with Dr. Sore Eyes upon return to New Mouse City. I shielded my eyes as I checked out the map. Just as I'd thought: We were in a place called the **All-Gold Woods**. And boy, was it all gold! The trees were gold, the leaves were gold, the grass was gold, the fruit was gold . . . even the flowers were gold! I noticed birds' nests made of gold in the trees, and there was a stream **FLOWING** with golden water.

The wind blew the leaves on the trees, making them ring like a thousand tinkling bells.

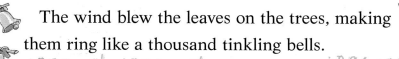

Ring! Ring! Ring! Ring! Ring! Ring! Ring! Ring!

It sounded just like an enormouse wind chime.

"Wow! I didn't know this land really existed. I thought it was only a **legend**," Boils commented.

"Have you ever seen such a **beautiful** sight?" Goose Blahblah asked. "Who doesn't love gold?"

But Oscar just scratched his head. "Why isn't there anyone around?" he asked. "We haven't seen **one** frog, **one** squirrel, **one** bird, or even **one** insect!"

The Land of Gold

Queen: Dorothy, Queen of Metal, She Who Sparkles, Treasure of Treasures, Gem of Gems, Jewel of All Jewels
Royal Palace: Sparkle Palace
Currency: Goldar
Spoken Language: Goldian
Information about the Land: There are no inhabitants in this land, because no one can live here. Keep reading to find out why.

Can you find the
CRYSTAL
KEY?

I nodded. Oscar was right. There was something strange about this place. *Something really strange!*

We continued down a GOLDEN path that led to Sparkle Palace. Along the way, we passed trees glittering with **EMERALDS** and DIAMONDS.

Goose Blahblah was in heaven. "Jewels, jewels, jewels! Every girl needs jewels!" she sang.

Just then one of the jewels fell out of a tree and hit me in the snout.

"Ow!" I complained. Then I saw that it wasn't a **jewel** that hit me. It was another CRYSTAL key. Soon we reached Sparkle Palace. I knocked but no one answered.

I **turned** the golden handle and went in.

May I come in?

Can you find the
CRYSTAL
KEY?

SORRY, CHARLIE

We were greeted by a golden statue.

"Welcome to the Land of Gold. I am Queen Dorothy. Why are you here?" she said in a robotic voice.

I felt *silly* talking to a statue, but what could I do? I introduced myself and said we were searching for the Heart of Happiness.

"Sorry, Charlie," the statue replied. "It's not here."

I was so disappointed I didn't even mind that the queen had called me the **wrong name**. I headed glumly for the door, absentmindedly picking up another CRYSTAL key I found on the floor.

"Wait!" the queen called. "Why don't you stay the night?"

Why not? I thought. All this searching was really wearing me out!

Suddenly, I heard something **growling**. I cringed. Was it a robotic guard dog? Was he **VICIOUS**? Would we have to pull out his batteries?

Then I noticed Oscar holding his stomach. "I'm hungry," he said, turning red.

We went to the kitchen. We saw a gold table, plates, glasses, and another CRYSTAL key.

Can you find the **CRYSTAL KEY?**

Spaghetti with cheese

Pizza

Frosted vanilla cake

A minute later, I heard more growling. This time it was coming from me!

I spotted a plate of spaghetti, a pizza, and a huge cake.

"**LET'S EAT!**" I said.

I bit into the pizza and screamed. It was made of jewels! The tomatoes were **RUBIES**, the olives were **EMERALDS**, and the mozzarella was made of DIAMONDS.

Goose Blahblah tried the spaghetti. But it was made of pure SILVER. The cake was made of *pearls*.

A stream of diamonds poured out of the faucet.

We decided to go to bed. But upstairs, my golden bed was as hard as ROCKS,

Can you find the **CRYSTAL KEY?**

and my gold blanket was **cold**. I rolled over and felt something poke me in the back. Was it a golden bedspring? No, it was just another CRYSTAL key.

I looked at the key. It was nice to have all these keys, but what about the *Heart of Happiness*? Would we ever find it?

That night I tried everything I could to help me fall asleep. I counted **SHEEP**. I counted **cheese puffs**. I counted sheep eating cheese puffs. But nothing worked! In the morning, I noticed that everyone else looked tired too.

What a night!

I didn't get a wink of sleep!

THE RICHEST CHAMELEON ON THE BLOCK

We said good-bye to the queen. She told us we could take anything we liked as a parting gift. So Goose Blahblah packed a trunk with *precious* stones. Boils filled a bag with GOLDEN coins.

"We're rich!" they yelled together.

They attached their treasure to the dragon with a rope. I was about to protest when I spotted something in the sand. Was it a DIAMOND? No, it was a CRYSTAL key.

Can you find the CRYSTAL KEY?

We traveled all day, but toward evening, a TERRIBLE storm blew in.

The dragon flapped his wings furiously, but the extra baggage weighed him down. We were losing **ALTITUDE** by the minute.

"We have to get rid of the trunk and the bag of GOLD before it's too late!" I yelled.

Quickly, I untied the rope. Precious stones and golden coins spilled out and then vanished from sight.

The dragon soared higher. We were safe! But Boils and Goose Blahblah were heartbroken.

"All that GOLD," Boils sobbed. "I was going to be the richest chameleon on the block."

Goose Blahblah nodded. "All those JEWELS," she moaned. "I could have worn a different gemstone every day of the year!"

While Boils and Goose Blahblah complained, the dragon landed on top of a **rocky** peak so we could rest.

It was a beautiful night. The sky was a **DEEP VELVETY BLUE** and the moon hung in the air like a precious slice of cheese. Oscar lay on his back, admiring the millions of *Stars* floating peacefully overhead.

"Ah, look at that view," he sighed. "Now, that is worth all the money in the world."

"But I love MONEY," Boils insisted.

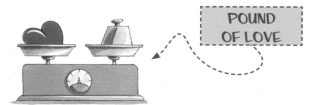

POUND OF LOVE

QUART OF FRIENDSHIP

YARD OF HAPPINESS

"Oh, Boils, MONEY can't buy everything," Oscar explained. "You can't buy a pound of *love* or a quart of *friendship* or a yard of *happiness*."

Boils grinned. "Well, at least you can buy **candy**," he said, pulling out a gold coin from his armpit. "Got anything, Sir Knight?"

I gave Boils his candy. Then I studied the map. **HOLEY CHEESE!** We had reached the **Land of Fairy Tales**.

The Land of Fairy Tales

THE LAND OF FAIRY TALES

I LOVE FAIRY TALES!

The next morning, we landed between the Little Mermaid Sea and the houses of the *Three Little Pigs*.

I was so excited! Did I mention I **LOVE** fairy tales?

The Land of Fairy Tales

King: In this land, there aren't any kings or queens.
Royal Palace: The Enchanted Palace
Currency: Golden Fablar
Spoken Language: Talebic
Information about the Land: The inhabitants are characters from fairy tales, fables, and legends from all over the world.

I couldn't believe we were walking right into some of my *favorite* storybook places. We passed the pond of **the Ugly Duckling** and **Little Red Riding Hood Woods**.

We had to drag Boils away from the witch's candy-covered house in **Hansel and Gretel Forest**. And Goose Blahblah almost pecked at a poison apple at the house of **Snow White and the Seven Dwarfs**.

Oscar made friends with a golden fish in **PINOCCHIO VILLAGE**, and I talked to an enchanted bluebird in *Sleeping Beauty Forest*.

Did I mention I love fairy tales?

ON TALKING BOOK PEAK

Still there was no sign of the *Heart of Happiness*.

Then Boils had an idea. "Let's climb **Talking Book Peak**. That book knows everything. It can tell us where to find the Heart of Happiness," he suggested.

By the **LIGHT** of the moon, we began our climb. The path was formed of rocks that were sculpted to look like letters of the alphabet.

"I will talk to the talking book," Goose Blahblah said.

"You!" snorted Boils. "It won't want to talk to a **chatterbox** like you."

"Sir Geronimo will talk to the book!" Oscar declared.

ME? TALK TO A BOOK?

I guess it made sense. Everyone knows I love books. I love READING them. I love **writing** them. I even love looking at them.

We climbed up the stone letters to the Talking Book. It was closed.

"Good evening, Mr. Book," I squeaked, feeling embarrassed. "May I ask you a question?"

At first nothing happened. Then the pages of the book began to **turn**. Fairies, witches, and elves fluttered out. As I watched in AMAZEMENT, something struck me in the snout. It was a CRYSTAL key.

Was the book trying to tell me something?

Can you find the
CRYSTAL
KEY?

WAS IT SOMETHING I SAID?

Suddenly, the Talking Book asked in a deep voice, "WHAT IS YOUR QUESTION?"

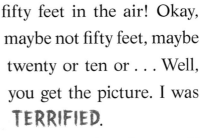

I was so scared I jumped fifty feet in the air! Okay, maybe not fifty feet, maybe twenty or ten or . . . Well, you get the picture. I was **TERRIFIED**.

I introduced myself and explained about the Heart of Happiness.

The book snapped shut. **Was it something I said?**

A second later, the

book said, "I will give you this information, but only if you pass a **TEST**."

My whiskers *shivered*. A test? Would I need a number two **PENCIL**? Would I lose points for bad **PawwRiting**?

The Talking Book interrupted my thoughts. "You must tell me a fable about something **important**," he said.

I felt a panic attack coming on. Then I remembered a fable my aunt Sweetfur had told me when I was a little **mouseling**. . . .

In the Land of Fairy Tales . . .

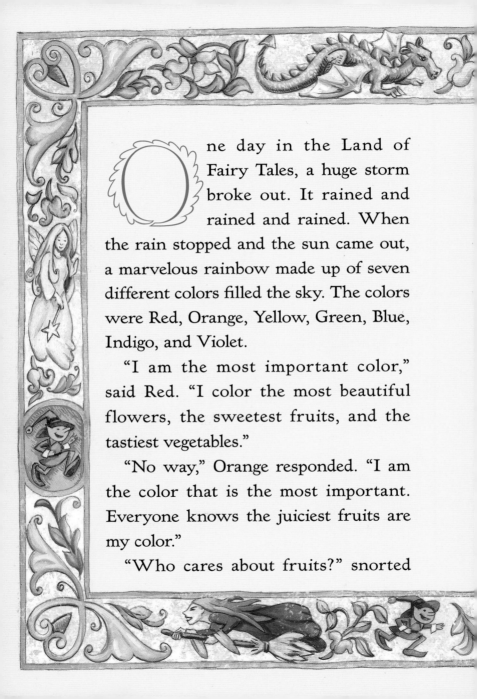

One day in the Land of Fairy Tales, a huge storm broke out. It rained and rained and rained. When the rain stopped and the sun came out, a marvelous rainbow made up of seven different colors filled the sky. The colors were Red, Orange, Yellow, Green, Blue, Indigo, and Violet.

"I am the most important color," said Red. "I color the most beautiful flowers, the sweetest fruits, and the tastiest vegetables."

"No way," Orange responded. "I am the color that is the most important. Everyone knows the juiciest fruits are my color."

"Who cares about fruits?" snorted

Yellow. "I am the most important color. I am the color of the sun!"

"I am the most important," Green insisted. "I color all of the plants on Earth!"

"Big deal," boomed Blue. "I am the color of the sky and the sea. That's way more important!"

"Oh yeah?" Indigo protested. "Without me, you wouldn't see the stars at night. Now that's important!"

"I'll tell you who's the most important — me!" Violet shrieked. "I hold up the rest of you!"

The colors argued and argued.

Suddenly, Red split away from the group. "I'm leaving," Red shouted. "I'm better off without all of you!"

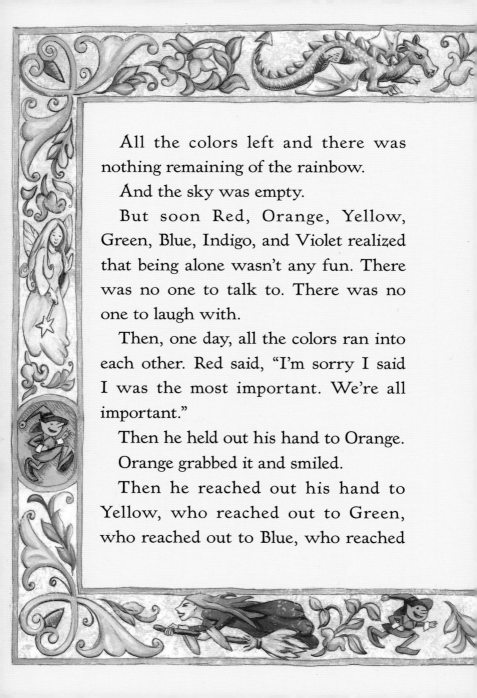

All the colors left and there was nothing remaining of the rainbow.

And the sky was empty.

But soon Red, Orange, Yellow, Green, Blue, Indigo, and Violet realized that being alone wasn't any fun. There was no one to talk to. There was no one to laugh with.

Then, one day, all the colors ran into each other. Red said, "I'm sorry I said I was the most important. We're all important."

Then he held out his hand to Orange.

Orange grabbed it and smiled.

Then he reached out his hand to Yellow, who reached out to Green, who reached out to Blue, who reached out to Indigo, who reached out to Violet.

As if by magic, a beautiful rainbow formed in the sky.

At last all seven colors of the rainbow were shining again in peace and harmony.

"I must say, we look great when we all work together," said Red.

And this time no one disagreed.

SWEET AND SAPPY

When I was finished with my story, I sat chewing my whiskers. Had I passed the test? I know the story I told was sort of **sweet** and *sappy*. Well, okay, it wasn't just sort of sweet. It was the kind of story that could give a mouse a toothache! But it was all I had.

The Talking Book began to leaf through his pages. Then he said, "Nice story, Geronimo. You have **passed** my test, so I will give you all the information you seek."

I was thrilled. This was it! At last we would find out where the Heart of Happiness was **hiding**! But then the Talking Book announced, "The Heart of Happiness cannot be found in the Land of Fairy Tales."

I was **crushed**. If the Heart of Happiness

wasn't in the Land of Fairy Tales, then we were done. There were no more lands left to explore. We'd have to go back to the Queen of the Fairies **empty-handed**.

We boarded the Dragon of the Rainbow with heavy

A NICE PEACEFUL NIGHT

That evening we stopped to rest. Oscar built a
FIRE, pitched a TENT, and made some delicious
hot chocolate. As I was sipping it, I found
another CRYSTAL key. How strange!

Then Oscar played his violin. I was IMPRESSED.
For a cockroach, Oscar was one WELL-ROUNDED bug.

We sang songs and chatted late into the night. It
seemed as if no one wanted to go to sleep. I guess

Can you find the CRYSTAL KEY?

we all knew that our **adventure** would soon be over. I looked around at all my friends in the Heart-Finders Club. The dragon lounged quietly on a rock, gazing up at the stars. Goose Blahblah was talking Snowy Dawn's ear off. **POOR THING!** Though it almost looked like the princess was smiling. Oscar was gathering **SOFT LEAVES** for us to sleep on, and Boils was on his tenth cup of hot cocoa.

It was nice to see everyone in the Heart-Finders Club getting along so well. I leaned back in the crook of a tree, enjoying the *peaceful* night.

Then Oscar suggested we play a game of charades.

"I'll go first!" Goose Blahblah insisted.

"Hey, what about me?" Boils complained. "Why can't I go first?"

Before long, the two were arguing away. I sighed. Yes, nothing like a *calm, peaceful* night.

Anyone want to play charades?

RETURN TO THE KINGDOM OF THE FAIRIES

The next morning we left at **dawn**. We flew and flew until we reached the Kingdom of the Fairies.

As the Dragon of the Rainbow descended toward the CRYSTAL landing pad, I found another CRYSTAL key. I tried to look on the bright side. Though I was disappointed

that I hadn't found the Heart of Happiness, at least I had found **something**.

I put my paw into my pocket and **jingled** all the CRYSTAL keys I had picked up during the trip. The night before, sitting under the tree, I had counted them. I had found *thirty-two* CRYSTAL keys. What were they for? Why did they seem to appear everywhere I went? Were they part of a **BIGGER RIDDLE**?

I stared up at the *star-filled* sky and wondered if I would ever learn the answers to my questions.

Can you find the CRYSTAL KEY?

THIRTY-THREE
CRYSTAL LOCKS

At that moment, I spotted a shooting star.

It zipped across the sky, lighting up the night. I made a wish. Why not? I had nothing to lose. "Please lead me to the Heart of Happiness," I whispered.

The star fell straight **DOWN**. Holey cheese! It landed right next to us on the GREAT CRYSTAL OAK in the Garden of Fairies.

"Let's follow it!" I yelled to my friends. As we were racing through the garden, I nearly tripped over another KEY. Make that thirty-three CRYSTAL KEYS!

The crystal garden **shimmered** in the moonlight. We passed a CRYSTAL pond with CRYSTAL lily pads and tiny CRYSTAL fish. There

were CRYSTAL rosebushes, CRYSTAL benches, a CRYSTAL wishing well, and even a CRYSTAL water fountain.

Blub!

But when I reached the CRYSTAL oak tree, I gasped. There between its roots was a small door with thirty-three CRYSTAL locks!

So that was what those *thirty-three* CRYSTAL KEYS were for!

So that was what the keys were for!

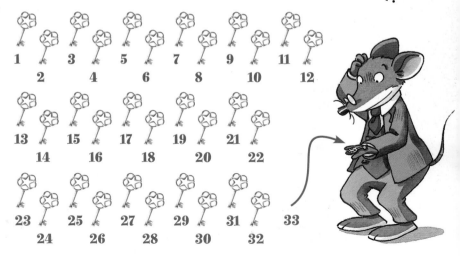

1 2 3 4 5 6 7 8 9 10 11 12
13 14 15 16 17 18 19 20 21 22
23 24 25 26 27 28 29 30 31 32 33

1

Between the roots of the oak,
a tiny, tiny, tiny door was hidden. . . .

With trembling paws, I took the keys and opened the locks **one by one**. Then, with the door half-open, I poked my head in and . . . fell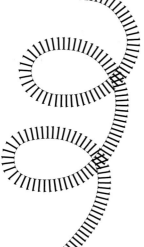

2

With the door half-open . . .

3

I poked my head in and fell!

I HATE ROLLER COASTERS!

Down, **down**, **down** I tumbled into the **darkness**.

I was on some kind of SLIPPERY SLIDE.

It felt like one of those scary roller-coaster rides at Mouseyland Amusement Park. Killer cat claws! I hate roller coasters!

"**HELP!**" I yelled at the top of my lungs.

Just then I hit bottom.

BRRR! It was cold. I looked around, straining to see in the dark. I was in a large, spooky cave.

My heart began to pound under my fur. Did I mention I'm not the **BRAVEST** mouse on the block? I'm afraid of spiders and snakes and those windup *chattering*

plastic teeth. And I'm afraid of ghosts and cats and the night. I chewed on my pawnails.

Oh, how did I get myself into such a **mess**? I was a good mouse. I said please and thank you. I ate my vegetables. Well, except for the time my cousin Trap tried to get me to eat pickled brussels sprouts. **Yuck!** The smell was enough to curl my whiskers!

The 𝕹𝕴𝕲𝕳𝕿 dragged on and on.

I was exhausted, but I couldn't sleep. I was too afraid!

A Ray of Light

Do you know what I learned while I was stuck in that cave? I learned that even scaredy-mice fall asleep. In the morning my own snoring woke me up!

At first I was embarrassed, but then I remembered I was alone in a **DARK, SPOOKY** cave. I stood up and stretched. I felt a little better, so I did a few **JUMPING JACKS**. I felt a little better, so I did a few **PUSH-UPS**. I felt a little better, so I *JOGGED* in place. Then I stubbed my toe. **Youch!** I took off my glasses so I could cry freely.

At that moment, a bright ray of sunlight lit up the cave. The cave was made of CRYSTAL! Now I felt a whole lot better.

The sun sparkled on the water of a large

spring in the center of the cave. A **WATERFALL** flowed into the spring, and a beautiful **rainbow** hung in the air.

ABOUT SUNLIGHT

Sunlight is responsible for lots of wonderful things. It makes plants grow, heats up the Earth, and provides us with vitamin D. Plus, being in the sunshine can make us feel happy and relaxed. If you are feeling down, try spending some time outside in the bright sunshine. It just might make you smile!

It was so dark. . . .
Where was I?

Suddenly, a light from above
pierced through the darkness. . . .

I was in a crystal cave!

The Mystery of the Seven Hearts

I moved closer to the spring and peered into the water. Cheese niblets! There, at the bottom of the spring, were seven hearts! One was GOLD. One was silver. One was amber. One was RUBY. One was sapphire. One was EMERALD. And one was a transparent CRYSTAL.

Could one of them be the Heart of Happiness? And how would I know which one? Then I saw words carved at the bottom of the spring:

Seven hearts you will see,
But only one will bring you glee.
So choose wisely, for if you're wrong,
Your happiness will soon be gone!

I was a wreck. Which heart was I supposed to choose? The gold one SHONE like the sun, but the silver one sparkled like the moon. Or maybe I was supposed to take the amber one, or the ruby one, or the sapphire, emerald, or crystal one. It was all so confusing. I'm not always the best at making decisions. Sometimes I have trouble picking out which pair of underwear to put on!

My paws shook as I reached for the seven glittering hearts. Each one seemed to be calling to me in a little squeaky voice: "Take me! Take me!"

Which heart should I choose?

Slimy Swiss rolls! Now I was hearing voices! I felt my forehead to make sure I wasn't coming down with something. What if I **FAINTED**? There was no one around to save me.

Snap out of it, Geronimo! I scolded myself. *You're here to choose a heart for the Queen of the Fairies.*

That got me thinking about the queen. Unlike some of the other kings and queens we had met, the Queen of the Fairies was **good** and KIND. Her castle wasn't made of GOLD or **silver** or some other precious stone.

She wasn't into money or **expensive** things. She didn't wear fancy ball gowns or drive a luxurious car. She didn't drape herself in jewels or insist on gourmet meals. Her castle was made of crystal, not diamonds. CRYSTAL. . . that was it! I was so excited I nearly fell into the water. At last I knew what to do.

I reached out my paw and grabbed the CRYSTAL heart.

As I held it, a ray of light struck the heart, and the heart reflected the seven colors of the **rainbow**.

This is the Heart of Happiness!

A Secret Passage!

I couldn't wait to present the Heart of Happiness to the queen. There was only one little problem. I was stuck in a CREEPY cave with no way out! What if I never got out? Headlines flashed before my eyes:

Publisher Perishes
in Crystal Cave!
Stilton's Skeleton Found
in Fantasy Land!

Just then I spotted NINE RIDDLES etched into the crystal above my head. It seemed that I had to solve the riddles to find a secret exit. Could I do it?

THE EXIT TO THE CAVE
IS CLOSE TO YOU!

A SEE-THROUGH WALL
SEPARATES YOU FROM IT,

A WALL THAT IS
CLEAN AND CLEAR.

BUT IF YOU WISH TO
FIND YOUR WAY OUT,

YOU MUST SOLVE THE
RIDDLES YOU HEAR.

THE FIRST LETTER
OF EACH ANSWER
WILL SPEED YOU ON YOUR WAY,

SO START SOLVING
THESE RIDDLES
BEFORE YOU'RE OLD AND GRAY!

1. 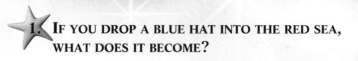 IF YOU DROP A BLUE HAT INTO THE RED SEA, WHAT DOES IT BECOME?

2. WHAT IS THE LARGEST ANT IN THE WORLD?

3. WHAT CAN YOU SERVE BUT NOT EAT?

4. WHAT CITY HAS NO PEOPLE?

5. WHAT IS ROUND AND NEVER HAS AN END TO IT?

6. WHAT DO YOU GET WHEN YOU CROSS A SNOWMAN WITH A WOLF?

7. WHAT BET CAN NEVER BE WON?

8. WHAT BUILDING HAS THE MOST STORIES?

9. WHAT IS SOMETHING YOU CAN'T EAT FOR DINNER?

THE EXIT TO THE CAVE IS CLOSE TO YOU!

SOLUTIONS: 1. WET 2. ANTARCTICA 3. TENNIS BALL 4. ELECTRICITY 5. RING 6. FROSTBITE 7. ALPHABET 8. LIBRARY 9. LUNCH

I racked my brain and finally solved all the riddles. The beginning letters of the **NINE ANSWERS** spelled out the word *waterfall*. "That's it!" I squeaked. "The exit to the cave is behind the **WATERFALL**!"

I poked my head through the **SEE-THROUGH WALL** of water, and it was just as I'd suspected. On the other side of

I reached out my paw ...

I poked my head to the other side of the waterfall ...

I crossed the waterfall ...

the waterfall was a CRYSTAL staircase!

I was so happy I could have DANCED up the CRYSTAL staircase. Too bad it was so LONG . . . and **STEEP** . . . and slippery. Cheese niblets! Would I make it? I kept my eyes glued to the sunny sky above me.

and on the other side was a crystal staircase that went up and up and up!

KEEP AWAY FROM CACKLE

After about a billion years, I made it to the top. My head popped out of the crystal well. Whew! I was exhausted. I felt like I had just done the stairmouster for two days straight. I needed a **cold** drink, a **snack**, and a **LOOOONG** nap.

But at that moment, an evil voice shrieked, "Give me the heart!"

The Dragon of Darkness soared overhead, with someone on its back. Rat-munching rattlesnakes! It was Cackle, the *Queen of the Witches*!

The dragon landed in the crystal garden.

Thinking fast, I threw the **HEART** into the CRYSTAL POND. It would be safe there.

The queen jumped off the dragon's back. "I know that you found the *Heart of Happiness*! Give it to me!" she yelled.

I tried to stay calm, but I was **shaking** inside. Have you ever been yelled at by a witch? Let me tell you, it can make your fur stand on **END**!

"I'm sorry, I don't have the *heart*," I said, putting on my bravest face. Cackle stamped her foot and waved her arms in the air.

"**Ridiculous**, mouse! You must think I was born yesterday! I know you have it. Now give it to me so I

can crush it to bits!" she demanded.

The queen ranted about how much she hated happiness. "Happy people always smile and laugh and DO NICE THINGS FOR OTHERS. It's disgusting,"

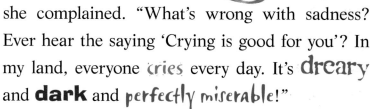

HAPPINESS Is . . .
Happiness is contagious! If you are happy and want to make others happy, show others the light you have in your heart! In a happy world, you live better: It is nicer to be surrounded by happy faces than by sad faces.

she complained. "What's wrong with sadness? Ever hear the saying 'Crying is good for you'? In my land, everyone cries every day. It's dreary and **dark** and perfectly miserable!"

Yikes! The Queen of the Witches was a little crazy. That's right: Cackle was cuckoo!

Now she stared **DEEP** into my eyes. "Enough STALLING, mouse. Give me that heart or the DRAGON OF DARKNESS will snap you up for a snack!" she threatened.

OSCAR UNDERSTOOD!

Suddenly, my friends arrived. Now if I could just get the **DRAGON OF DARKNESS** to stop **breathing** down my neck. I wondered if he had brushed his TEETH in the past century.

Oscar yelled, "Do you have the *Heart of Happiness*?"

When the queen turned, I pointed to the pond. Then I said, "No!"

Oscar nodded. He understood that I had **hidden** the heart in the pond.

The Queen of the Witches grew FURIOUS. "I've had it with your silly games!" she screeched. She signaled to the dragon. Before I could squeak, he **GRABBED** me with his RAZOR-SHARP talons and took off.

HIGHER and HIGHER we flew until my friends were just tiny spots down below. Rotten Swiss rolls! Could things get any **worse**?

Two minutes later, the dragon let go and I plunged HEADFIRST toward the ground.

Oscar understood!

THANKS FOR SAVING MY LIFE!

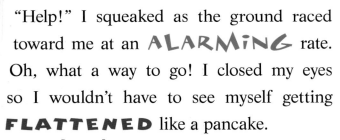

"Help!" I squeaked as the ground raced toward me at an ALARMING rate. Oh, what a way to go! I closed my eyes so I wouldn't have to see myself getting FLATTENED like a pancake.

Then a miracle happened. Something broke my fall. I opened my eyes. I was sitting on the back of a white unicorn with shimmering rainbow-colored wings.

"Wow!" I said. "Thanks for saving my life!"

The unicorn smiled and shook his long mane. "No problemo," he neighed. "My name is Rocket."

As we flew back toward my friends, Rocket told me about himself.

★ ROCKET'S STORY

I was born in the Land of the Unicorns, in a happy valley north of the Golden Mountains, in the Kingdom of Fantasy.

One day the Queen of the Witches, who was jealous of Blossom, set off a tremendous windstorm that destroyed the castle of the fairies.

Blossom fainted and was trapped under the rubble. I dug her out and put her on my back.

Then I began to run. The storm followed me, roaring and tugging at my tail, but I kept going. I had to save the queen.

My heart pounded and my throat burned, but I didn't stop. I ran and ran and ran until I was dripping in sweat. In the end, I beat out the storm. Blossom was saved!

When she came to, Blossom was so thankful she wanted to reward me. She said, "If you could have anything in the world, what would it be?"

I had always dreamed of having wings, so I told the queen, "I would love to have wings. I could fly as fast as a rocket."

So Blossom gave me these amazing wings. "From now on you will be named Rocket," she said. And, well, not to brag or anything, but now I really am as fast as a rocket.

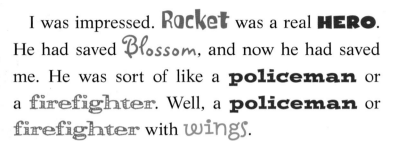

I was impressed. **Rocket** was a real **HERO**. He had saved **Blossom**, and now he had saved me. He was sort of like a **policeman** or a firefighter. Well, a **policeman** or firefighter with wings.

I wanted to **reward** him. But it wasn't like I had a spare pair of wings in my pocket. Then I remembered something I did have.

"Candy?" I offered. **Rocket** gobbled it up.

ROCKET

A snowy-white winged unicorn. He flies really fast, because his wings were made with fairies' breath. His luminous horn has great powers: Whoever touches it is cured of every ailment. He is the guardian of the Kingdom of the Fairies and is the most trusted servant of Blossom, whom he protects from anyone who wishes her harm.

I'VE GOT IT!

Rocket approached the *Garden of Fairies,* where my friends were waiting for me. I spotted Cackle climbing back onto her dragon.

"It doesn't end here, rodent!" she screeched. "We'll meet again!"

I stared at the dragon as it flew off into the sky. **WHO KNOWS?** I thought. Maybe we would see each other again someday.

As soon as **Rocket** landed, Oscar ran up to me. He was practically jumping out of his shell with excitement.

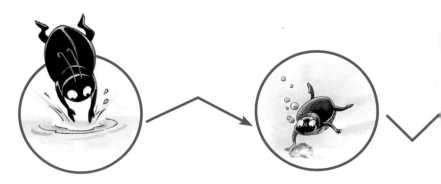

"I've got it! I've got the *Heart of Happiness*! After you left, I dove into the pond where you pointed. The heart was right there. It got a little **muddy**, but I rinsed it off and now **LOOK**!" He beamed.

The HEART OF CRYSTAL shone brightly.

I was so relieved. After all we'd been through, it would have been **awful** to lose the heart.

"Hooray for the *Heart-Finders Club*!" I squeaked. Everyone cheered, including **Rocket**. "You're part of our club now, too," I told the unicorn. Then we all came **together** in a group hug.

A SPECIAL FAMILY

Suddenly, Snowy burst into **tears**.

"Why are you crying?" I asked her.

She dried her tears. "I'm crying because I'm so **happy** to have friends who love me," she explained. Then she finally told us her **STORY**.

SNOWY'S STORY

My father was the king of a faraway and happy land, the Kingdom of Ice. One day it started to snow, and it snowed for seven hundred days and seven hundred nights. Everyone would have died of hunger beneath the snow, but my father had a ship built. All of our people, the Snow People, boarded the ship in search of a new land where we could live in peace. We sailed for days, weeks, and months. Then, when we were in the Sea of Dreams, a storm broke out.

My father ordered everyone belowdecks, and he locked the hatches and the portholes. Someone, however, was left outside: me! I was small and no one noticed me. No one heard my cries. A wave swept me away and I fell into the Sea of Dreams. But two talons grabbed me and saved me. It was the Dragon of the Rainbow. He brought me to the Kingdom of the Fairies. Since then, I have been too sad to speak.

The Stilton Family

It was great to finally hear Snowy's story. I gave her a warm hug.

"We are your special family now," I said to her. Then I told her about my own special family. Not everyone knows it, but the Stilton family adopted ME when I was a young mouselet and gave me a loving home. I grew up with my sister, Thea; my cousin Trap; my grandpa William Shortpaws; and my aunt Sweetfur.

"Families are formed in all different ways," I told Snowy.

THE MATHEMATICS OF HAPPINESS

If you divide your happiness with others, you are really **multiplying** it! If you get angry for a minute, you subtract sixty seconds of happiness from your life!

"The important thing is that you all care about each other. That's what makes a home happy! The best kind of home is a place where you feel LOVED!" I squeaked.

"And a place with lots of **candy**!" Boils giggled.

"And a place where you can **talk** all day!" Goose Blahblah blabbed.

"And a place where no one screams, 'Squash that bug!'" Oscar said.

"And a place where you can spread your wings!" Rocket added.

"And a place with lots of FRIENDS!" the Dragon of the Rainbow sang.

AN EXPLOSION OF STARS!

I turned the *Heart of Happiness* over in my paws. I was feeling happy and warm. Strangely, the crystal heart felt warm, too. For a minute I felt like a mother hen warming her baby chick.

Then a ray of sunlight hit the crystal, causing an EXPLOSION OF STARS.

"**WOW!**" my friends cried.

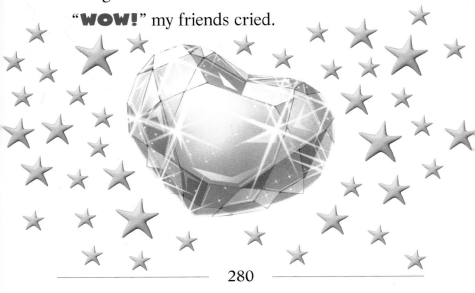

But I was a little worried. What if the *Heart of Happiness* **burst into bits** before we made it back?

Was I holding a ticking time bomb?

"Let's go!" I squeaked, scampering toward the Crystal Castle.

I didn't stop until I reached the queen.

I bowed before her. "Here it is, Your Majesty," I squeaked. "Just as you requested, it's the *Heart of Happiness.*" I held out the crystal heart.

I was feeling **EXTRA-PROUD** of myself and of

all my friends in the Heart-Finders Club. After all, we had just battled a *hideous* ogre, scaled a **treacherous** mountain, outsmarted a *snooty* king, and escaped from a TERRIFYING witch, all for the Heart of Happiness.

"Thank you," Queen Blossom said with a smile.

Then she turned to one of the fairies in her court and said, "Please bring the heart back to the Crystal Cave."

Why?

I was in shock. Had the queen **lost her marbles**? "But why would you do that?" I whined. "It was so hard to find."

"The important thing is not **FINDING** the heart, dear knight," the queen said. "The important thing is **searching** for it."

I looked at my friends and thought about our adventure. Blossom was right. Happiness isn't something you can hold. It is something you feel. It can be found inside you.

The queen pulled out an OFFICIAL-LOOKING scroll. "I am happy to nominate you *Ambassador of Happiness*!" she proclaimed.

Ambassador
of Happiness

I, Blossom,
Queen of the Fairies,
nominate

Geronimo Stilton

AMBASSADOR OF
HAPPINESS!

Signed:
Blossom

A DIP IN THE RAINBOW!

It was time to go home. I hugged my friends and climbed back onto the Dragon of the Rainbow.

The dragon lifted his mighty wings and took off into the air. I didn't even let out one squeak. I was getting pretty good at this *flying* stuff. Still, I never did talk to the dragon about my Seat belt idea. Oh, well. Maybe on my next adventure.

I was feeling pretty relaxed when suddenly the

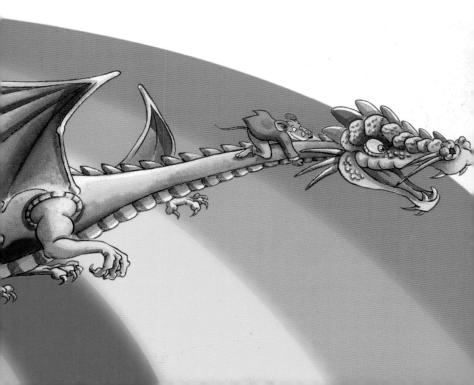

dragon dipped himself headfirst into the end of the *swirling* rainbow.

RATS! What was I saying about feeling relaxed? My whiskers **whirled** in fright. My heart **hammered** in my throat. I felt like I was getting sucked into a giant vacuum cleaner!

I tried to hang on to the dragon's neck but my paws were so sweaty I slipped.

"**Hellllllp!**" I squeaked.

Help . . . what is happening???

Help . . . what is happening???

Help . . . what is happening???

Help . . . What is happening???

Help . . . What is happening???

WHAT HAPPENED?

Suddenly, I found myself back home. I was in my **comfy**, cozy bed.

"Wh-wh-what's going on? Wh-wh-what **happened?**"

I stammered.

What happened?

Just then my alarm clock rang. It was seven in the morning.

I scratched my head. Then it hit me.

It had all been a dream!

Yes, my adventure in the Kingdom of Fantasy and the Quest for Paradise was only a dream.

Then I remembered the 101 plates of spaghetti I had eaten the night before. I rubbed my SWOLLEN stomach. The indigestion must have gotten to me. I always have crazy dreams when my stomach is upset. YUCK! I never wanted to see another plate of spaghetti again in my whole life!

I stretched my paws, put on my slippers, and shuffled into the bathroom.

I couldn't wait to take a nice HOT shower. Ahh! After a long shower, I brushed my teeth and got dressed.

The sun is coming up!

La la la!

La la la!

Then I looked at myself in the mirror. Same old face, but there was something different about my eyes. **They sparkled!**

For a minute, I thought I had SOAP BUBBLES in my eyes, but then I realized why my **EYES** were

Dum de doo . . .

dum-dum . . .

yes-sir-ee!

Life is beautiful,

and I am happy!

sparkling. Did you ever notice that when you're happy, your eyes SHINE? Well, I was happy. In fact, I couldn't wait to start my day! And that was really strange, because I usually HATE the morning!

SMILE! SMILE! SMILE!
When you get up in the morning, look at yourself in the mirror and smile. Even if you're not feeling happy, smiling can make you feel like a new mouse! Just brush back your fur, put your best paw forward, and smile, smile, smile! Oh, and don't forget to brush your teeth!

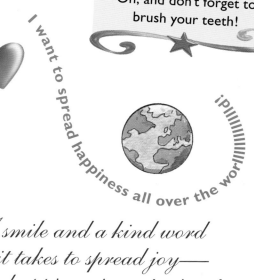

I want to spread happiness all over the world!!!!!!!!!

A smile and a kind word is all it takes to spread joy— because happiness is contagious!

It's Contagious!

Before I left my house, I said good-bye to my **little red fish**, Hannibal. He was swimming around and around in his CRYSTAL bowl.

"Have a great day, Hannibal. You're looking **SUPERFAST** today!" I squeaked happily.

Hannibal brought his face near the edge of the bowl. I couldn't say for sure, but he actually looked like he was *smiling*.

I left the house and picked up a paper at the newsstand. Bobby, the newspaper dealer, looked **glum**, so I told him a few

jokes. He was still laughing as I headed to my favorite diner, the Squeak & Chew.

Inside, I found the owner, Flip, frowning because he had BURNED some pancakes.

"I'll take them," I told Flip, grinning. "Just pour on the syrup."

Flip grinned back. This *happiness thing* was kind of FUN.

After I left the diner, I jumped onto a bus. An old lady boarded after me. "Why is it so **crowded**?" she grumbled. I smiled and gave her my seat. "Thank you, sonny!" she said, *smiling* back.

At last I reached my office at The Rodent's Gazette. My staff looked **tired**. "How about we order PIZZA for lunch?" I suggested. "My treat!"

Everyone **cheered**.

That night on my way home, I passed lots of sad-looking rodents. I smiled at everyone. And can you guess what happened?

Everyone answered me with a **smile**.

Yes, this happiness thing wasn't just fun, **it was contagious!**

I Love My Ducky!

Back at home, I made a nice, hot BUBBLE BATH. Oh, how I love my baths! When I was little, I spent hours in the tub playing with my rubber ducky. Now, of course, I just love the baths. Well, okay, I still love my ducky.

I was relaxing in the tub when I came up with an idea.

Mmmmmm ...

I would **write** a book about the Kingdom of Fantasy. I would write about the witches, Queen Chocolatina, Cackle, and the *Heart-Finders Club*. And of course, I would write about my **Quest for Paradise**.

I was so excited I jumped out of the tub, ran to the computer, and didn't stop TYPING until the book was finished. Well, okay, maybe I stopped once or twice for a **cheese** break, but you get the idea. . . .

Hooray! I am the Ambassador of Happiness!

ABOUT THE AUTHOR

 Born in New Mouse City, Mouse Island, **GERONIMO STILTON** is Rattus Emeritus of Mousomorphic Literature and of Neo-Ratonic Comparative Philosophy. For the past twenty years, he has been running *The Rodent's Gazette*, New Mouse City's most widely read daily newspaper.

Stilton was awarded the Ratitzer Prize for his scoops on *The Curse of the Cheese Pyramid* and *The Search for Sunken Treasure*. He has also received the Andersen 2000 Prize for Personality of the Year. One of his bestsellers won the 2002 eBook Award for world's best ratlings' electronic book. His works have been published all over the globe.

In his spare time, Mr. Stilton collects antique cheese rinds and plays golf. But what he most enjoys is telling stories to his nephew Benjamin.

And don't miss any of my other fabumouse adventures!

#1 LOST TREASURE OF THE EMERALD EYE

#2 THE CURSE OF THE CHEESE PYRAMID

#3 CAT AND MOUSE IN A HAUNTED HOUSE

#4 I'M TOO FOND OF MY FUR!

#5 FOUR MICE DEEP IN THE JUNGLE

#6 PAWS OFF, CHEDDARFACE!

#7 RED PIZZAS FOR A BLUE COUNT

#8 ATTACK OF THE BANDIT CATS

#9 A FABUMOUSE VACATION FOR GERONIMO

#10 ALL BECAUSE OF A CUP OF COFFEE

#11 IT'S HALLOWEEN, YOU 'FRAIDY MOUSE!

#12 MERRY CHRISTMAS, GERONIMO!

#13 THE PHANTOM OF THE SUBWAY

#14 THE TEMPLE OF THE RUBY OF FIRE

#15 THE MONA MOUSA CODE

#16 A CHEESE-COLORED CAMPER

#17 WATCH YOUR WHISKERS, STILTON!

#18 SHIPWRECK ON THE PIRATE ISLANDS

#19 MY NAME IS STILTON, GERONIMO STILTON

#20 SURF'S UP, GERONIMO!

#21 THE WILD, WILD WEST

#22 THE SECRET OF CACKLEFUR CASTLE

A CHRISTMAS TALE

#23 VALENTINE'S DAY DISASTER

#24 FIELD TRIP TO NIAGARA FALLS

#25 THE SEARCH FOR SUNKEN TREASURE

#26 THE MUMMY WITH NO NAME

#27 THE CHRISTMAS TOY FACTORY

#28 WEDDING CRASHER

#29 DOWN AND OUT DOWN UNDER

#30 THE MOUSE ISLAND MARATHON

#31 THE MYSTERIOUS CHEESE THIEF

CHRISTMAS CATASTROPHE

#32 VALLEY OF THE GIANT SKELETONS

#33 GERONIMO AND THE GOLD MEDAL MYSTERY

#34 GERONIMO STILTON, SECRET AGENT

#35 A VERY MERRY CHRISTMAS

#36 GERONIMO'S VALENTINE

#37 THE RACE ACROSS AMERICA

#38 A FABUMOUSE SCHOOL ADVENTURE

#39 SINGING SENSATION

#40 THE KARATE MOUSE

#41 MIGHTY MOUNT KILIMANJARO

#42 THE PECULIAR PUMPKIN THIEF

#43 I'M NOT A SUPERMOUSE!

#44 THE GIANT DIAMOND ROBBERY

If you like my brother's books,
check out these exciting
Thea Sisters adventures!

Geronimo Stilton

Thea Stilton
AND THE
MOUNTAIN OF FIRE

SCHOLASTIC

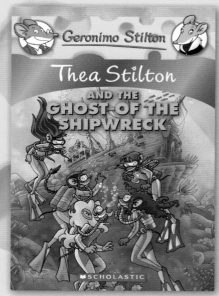

Geronimo Stilton

Thea Stilton
AND THE
GHOST OF THE
SHIPWRECK

SCHOLASTIC

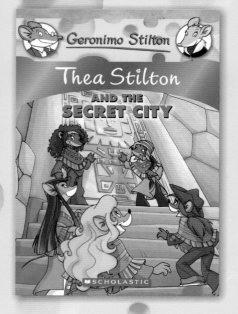

Geronimo Stilton

Thea Stilton
AND THE
SECRET CITY

SCHOLASTIC

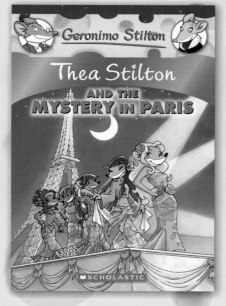

Geronimo Stilton

Thea Stilton
AND THE
MYSTERY IN PARIS

SCHOLASTIC

Listen to a Double Dose of Geronimo's "Fabumouse" Adventures on Audio!

Geronimo Stilton
Books 17 & 18

WATCH YOUR WHISKERS, STILTON!

SHIPWRECK ON THE PIRATE ISLANDS

Read by Bill Lobley

UNABRIDGED • 2 COMPACT DISCS

MORE 2-AUDIOBOOK PACKS AVAILABLE NOW:

WRITTEN BY *Geronimo Stilton*   READ BY *Bill Lobley*

And don't miss my first exciting journey through the Kingdom of Fantasy!

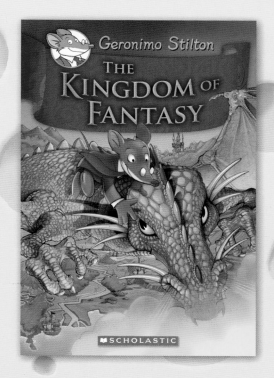

Spread happiness with a smile!